STICKS AND STONES

DONNA SHELTON

SADDLEBACK
EDUCATIONAL PUBLISHING

GRAVEL ROAD

Bi-Normal

Edge of Ready

Expecting *(rural)*

Falling Out of Place

FatherSonFather

Finding Apeman *(rural)*

A Heart Like Ringo
  Starr *(verse)*

I'm Just Me

Otherwise *(verse)*

Roadside Attraction *(rural)*

Rodeo Princess *(rural)*

Screaming Quietly

Self. Destructed.

Skinhead Birdy

Sticks and Stones *(rural)*

Teeny Little Grief
  Machines *(verse)*

That Selfie Girl *(verse)*

2 Days

Unchained

Varsity 170

SADDLEBACK
EDUCATIONAL PUBLISHING
www.sdlback.com

ISBN-13: 978-1-68021-103-0
ISBN-10: 1-68021-103-X
eBook: 978-1-63078-400-3

Printed in China
NOR/0316/CA21600430

20 19 18 17 16   1 2 3 4 5

CHAPTER 1

I lock myself in the bathroom. I feel sick. A queasiness in my stomach I have never felt before. It's not just in my stomach. It's somewhere deep inside me. I can't put it into words. I sit on the side of the bathtub listening to the noises outside the door. The footsteps descending the creaking stairs. The front door closing. The sound of a car's engine. The scatter of gravel as it drives away.

I'm staring at the toilet. Any second now, I'll throw up. I can feel it. I put my hands on my stomach, trying to settle the queasy flipping feeling. The feeling is growing stronger the more I try to ignore it. I know I should do something. Say something to someone. Have another person here with me, if only to hold my hair back as I throw up. I want to call someone. But my phone is all the way upstairs in my room. My legs are so weak. There's no way I can make the trip up all those stairs.

I keep replaying it all in my head. Plus all the things that lead up to it. All the things I could have done differently. I think of those TV shows Mom watches. There's one that specifically focuses on sex crimes. I remember watching those shows, saying she shouldn't have done that … she should have done this … if that were me …

I've just become an episode.

Tonight I understand how it's always so easy to say what I *would* do if I were put in a certain situation. But it's different when it actually happens. I know this now. I'm supposed to call someone. Call someone and say what? I've been raped? No. I can't say those words to another person. Saying those words will make it real. *I can't make it real.* Right here, right now, I feel safe in this little room. Nobody knows what happened. Nobody has to know.

I'm supposed to go to the hospital. There's something called a rape kit that doctors use to gather evidence. I remember that much from the show. I wish I'd paid more attention.

I should call the police, but I can't. I feel dirty. I can still feel him on my skin. I can smell him, a sultry mix of sweat and spicy cologne. I can feel the stickiness between my legs. It feels like bugs are crawling all over me. I can feel the heat from his mouth on me. I can feel his breath, reeking of beer.

I need it to stop.

I lunge forward. Grab on to the toilet with both hands and hurl. Before I can catch my breath, I heave again. My stomach cramps. I purge everything. The acid burns as it comes out through my nose, making it impossible to breathe. I heave again. This time so hard my bladder empties, soaking my panties. Urine runs down my legs.

I close my eyes. Blindly grab for the toilet paper to wipe my mouth. I spit the vile taste out. Wipe my mouth with wads of toilet paper. Drop the paper into the toilet. I close the lid and flush.

I sit here and stare at the shower curtain. I don't want to move. But I have to. I'm filthy. I smell of him. The bugs are crawling and burrowing into my thighs. I can smell beer, even with the smell of vomit searing my nostrils.

I get up. Pull the shower curtain aside. Turn on the water as hot as I can bear. I tear my clothes off and step into the tub. The water burns my skin as I wash him off me. My skin is turning red and it hurts. But I have to get rid of every trace of him. I have to feel clean again. I grab a bar of soap and scrub my body.

I scrub and scrub and scrub until I have no feeling. I scrub between my legs until the bugs stop crawling. I scrub until I'm sure I've drawn blood. The physical pain I'm inflicting on myself distracts me from the mental pain.

My eyes hurt.

My nostrils burn.

Any second now I hope the tears will flow. I can relieve my eyes of this ache. My head hurts. My eyes hurt in a way that only crying will relieve. I want to cry. Why can't I cry?

I use my dirty clothes to wipe up the wet floor. I wrap myself in a towel. Grab the mouthwash to rinse the horrible taste out of my mouth. With my toothbrush I brush every tooth until my gums bleed. I scrub my tongue until it's sore. Then I rinse with more mouthwash until all I can taste is mint.

I go upstairs to my room. My hair is wet. Sticking to my shoulders. I can feel cold beads of water running down my back.

I feel different.

I pull the sheets off my bed and stuff them into the hamper. Then I stuff my dirty clothes into it too.

Did this really happen? Did I imagine it all?

I notice the smell. My room smells like sex. It smells like his cologne. It smells as if something bad has happened here. I can't let Mom smell my room. If she smells my room, she will know.

She can *never* know.

I turn on my ceiling fan. Open my windows. A crisp breeze blows in. I feel cold. The smell should be gone before Mom gets home.

I go down the hall to Mom's room. Open the door. Look into the brightly lit space. I take Mom's robe from the back of her door. Wrap myself in it. It's soft and clean and smells like her cucumber bodywash. I toss the wet towel into her hamper. Look over to her bed.

Her bed is so comfortable and welcoming, with its

shiny green comforter covered with pink and white flowers. Matching pillows rest against the headboard. I crawl into the bed. Curl up into these pillows. I can remember being sandwiched between Mom and Dad all those years ago when they were still together. Monsters never came into my parents' room. Nothing can hurt me in here. I'm safe here.

╊

When I open my eyes, the room is dark. I can hear noises downstairs. The TV is on. I hear Mom's favorite TV show. Clinking noises come from the kitchen. A faint smell of chicken wafts upstairs.

Mom is home.

A part of me wants to run into the safety of her arms. But I'm afraid if I do, she'll automatically know what has happened. She can never know. I get up and go to my room to dress. A glance at the clock tells me jammies will do. My room is cold from having the windows open for hours. It's disinfected now of his smell. Purified with cold air.

I go downstairs. Mom is pulling something from the oven. It's my favorite dish: baked chicken breast smothered in mushroom sauce. My nostrils take in the scent, and my stomach rumbles with rejection. My senses are telling me how delicious Mom's chicken is. How good it will feel in an empty stomach. My stomach says, don't you dare.

"Hey, sleepyhead," she calls before I appear in the doorway of the kitchen. "Are you hungry?"

Not really. But I know I should try to eat just a little to avoid suspicion. Avoid suspicion of what? Mom has no reason to be suspicious of anything, but I feel as if she has. That's because I know something she doesn't.

Something has been taken from me. She'll notice. Maybe some food will help. Bring me out of my daze. Help me think. Or help me forget.

"I'll have a little."

She looks at me. "Did you eat earlier?" Knowing this is my favorite dish, she looks at me with some concern.

"Yeah, I did." I feel the need to over explain, like I do when I lie to her. "Cassie and I shared a pizza after school."

She nods and pulls two plates out of the cabinet. "Any big plans this weekend?"

She doesn't know about the date. I never told her about him because I know she would never approve of the relationship. Several years ago she used to work with his dad. They had a relationship that didn't end well. She never went into detail about it. I never asked. I just know she would never approve of me having a relationship with her ex-boyfriend's son.

I'm distracted by the voices on the TV. I hear a woman giving the details of her rape to two detectives. I go into the kitchen. Get silverware from the drawer.

"Can we watch something else?"

She laughs and hands me a plate. "I'm sure we can find something we both can agree on."

We bring our plates to the living room and sit on the couch. I take the remote and look through the cable guide as Mom brings us sodas and napkins.

I pick at my food. Chew on a small bite, then spit it out into a napkin. I play around with my knife and fork. Cut the food up. Take small bites that I end up spitting out into the napkin.

I can't seem to swallow the food. My throat won't let me. Mom doesn't notice. Eventually I give up and dump my food into the trash can. Then I come back to sit with her. I'm looking at the TV. But I don't know what's happening. I'm physically here, but my mind is far away.

CHAPTER 2

I wake up on the couch the next morning. It takes me a moment to realize where I am. The birds outside are chirping as daylight breaks. A crisp wind comes in through an open window.

I pull the blanket over me. Mom must have covered me with it last night. This is my first time waking up before the sun on a Saturday morning. I lie here and listen to the birds. Their lives are happy. Free.

I roll onto my back. Stare at the ceiling. Mom is still sleeping upstairs. She's blissfully unaware of the life-altering thing that happened in the room down the hall. This morning's haze makes me wonder if I imagined it all.

Are my memories of yesterday real? Did I blow it out of proportion?

I sit up and my stomach cramps. I press my stomach hard with my hands, as if that will make the cramps go away. But it doesn't.

When I finally manage to peel myself off the couch, I

go upstairs to my room. Everything is how I left it. I pull out some fresh sheets from a drawer. Make my bed. The sheets are crisp and clean, with a scent of lavender. I inhale, finally erasing his smell. I take my wastebasket and tidy up the room. My stomach cramps again, triggering a memory.

ᘖ

I can feel his hot wet skin against me. My stomach hurts as he slams into me with his hips. He's so heavy. I can barely breathe.

"Get off me," I gasp between thrusts. "Brad, stop!"

"Hold on, I'm almost done," he says.

I push at him, but he's determined to finish what he has started. I feel like he's stabbing me with a dull knife. Slowly cutting me. Reopening the wound again and again.

"Get off! Stop!"

He grabs my wrists. Pins them above my head. His body weighs me down. I can't move. His hips slam into mine. There are sharp pains in my stomach. Sweat drips off his forehead and into my eyes. I can't see. Can't breathe. I want to pass out. I'm praying that I will just pass out. Then his body turns rigid with one last thrust. He lets out a groan.

I feel as if my body is filled with filth.

I'm dirty. The kind of dirty I can never wash off. He leans down. Shoves his tongue into my mouth. His saliva fills my dry mouth with beer and sweat. Then he rolls over. Lies down beside me for a moment. I can finally breathe again. My lungs expand. My hands automatically go down between my legs. I'm wet with a mixture of sweat and blood. I want to retch.

It hurts.

My stomach hurts.

My legs hurt.

Is it supposed to hurt like this?

ೞ

I check the wastebasket, looking for a small square wrapper. I look underneath my bed. All over the floor. There's nothing. I don't remember him taking the time to put one on at all. My heart thuds hard in my chest when I realize he didn't use a condom.

I do the math in my head, trying to remember my last period. Trying to remember what they taught us in health class about ovulation and the menstrual cycle. If my calculations are correct, I'm in trouble.

I grab my phone. Open my web browser. Search for ways to prevent pregnancy. A drug called Plan B pops up. I've heard of this before in a commercial or something. I Google it. Looks like most pharmacies carry the pill, and it's available without a prescription. This one pill will prevent pregnancy if taken within seventy-two hours of having unprotected sex. The only downside is the price. It costs fifty dollars. I don't have fifty dollars.

I hurry and get dressed as quietly as I can. It's still

early. I don't want to wake Mom. I look through my purse and find my wallet. Eleven dollars and some change.

Not enough.

I go downstairs and pull the coin jar out of the cabinet. It's heavy. But there are mostly pennies. There's a Coinstar at the grocery store. I can trade the change for cash. See what I have to work with. I empty the jar into a baggie.

As I'm putting the baggie into my purse, I see Mom's purse on the counter. I stare at it, knowing she has money inside. How long will it take her to realize the money is gone? What kind of excuse can I give for stealing money from her? I don't want to steal her money, but I'm desperate.

I dig through her purse. Pull out her wallet. She has more than enough cash, but I can't take it all. I do the math in my head. My eleven dollars plus what is possibly in the coin jar equals—screw it! I'll take two twenties and return what's left.

As I'm putting her wallet back, I see her car keys. I only have my learner's permit, but I know how to drive. As long as I don't get caught, I should be okay. Taking the car will be a lot faster than walking to where I have to go. I guess right now it's go big or go home. Mom will be mad if she catches me, but I'll figure out how to deal with her when the time comes.

By the time I get to the store, I have an hour before the pharmacy opens. I go to the Coinstar. Empty my baggie into the tray. Watch the counter as the coins pour into the machine and the numbers tally up on the screen. Just short of twelve dollars. I print up my receipt and claim the money at the customer service desk.

With the money in my hand, I walk across the store. I'm the first customer in line at the pharmacy when it opens. The redheaded pharmacist looks like she's fresh out of college. She smiles at me as I approach the counter.

"Good morning, how may I help you?"

I look behind her at the shelves of drugs. I look around me to make sure I am out of earshot from any early morning shoppers.

"Hi, um … do you carry …" Was it just us? I quickly glance around again. "The Plan B pill?"

Her smile fades. "Yes, we do. Are you at least seventeen years old?"

No, but I nod anyway.

"May I see an ID?"

My heart sinks. I'm about to get busted. Didn't expect to get carded. I reach into my purse. Pull out my school ID. Slide it across the counter hoping for a miracle. She looks at it and back to me. She seems to be hesitating, which makes me nervous.

"I can't sell this to you. You have to be seventeen."

"I'll be seventeen in four months. Please?" I'm hoping she will take pity on me.

"I'm sorry, I can't. It would be against the law for me to sell this to you without a prescription or parental consent."

"The website says I don't need one."

"You need a prescription when you're under seventeen. You need a parent to take you to your doctor."

I feel like I'm going to cry. My eyes burn, but no tears will come. If I squeeze out a few tears, will it help her take pity on me and give me the pill?

"Look," she lowers her voice. "Go to the public health clinic. They're open until noon today. You don't need an appointment or a parent, just walk in. Someone there will be able to help you."

I can feel myself blushing from embarrassment. I nod hopelessly and hurry out the door.

Mom will be awake soon, if she's not already. I still need an excuse for stealing her money and taking the car.

CHAPTER 3

On the way home, I stop by McDonald's. Buy Mom some breakfast. When I get home, she's in the shower. I take the two twenties and put them back into her wallet. Then I put everything back exactly as I found it, hoping she won't notice. As I'm returning her keys, she walks into the kitchen in her bathrobe.

"Did you take the car?"

She has that scolding tone in her voice. She's not happy with me.

"Um, yeah." I show her the McDonald's bag. "I wanted to surprise you with breakfast."

She looks at me suspiciously and then sighs. "You don't have your license yet. If you get pulled over, you would be in trouble."

"I know. I was careful."

"That doesn't make it okay." She puts her hands on her hips, as if she's going to scold me further and then changes her mind. She takes the bag of food. Looks into it. "Thank you. It's a nice surprise. Just don't do it again."

Relief washes over me as I head to the stairs. I expected her to be furious with me, but she's not. I don't know how I got so lucky.

"Wait," she says. "You're not eating with me?"

My heart thuds hard in my chest for a moment. I scramble for an excuse. "I finished mine on the way home. It smelled too good. I couldn't wait."

She's about to say something, then stops. "Okay."

I go to my room and close the door. I sit down on my bed. I want to shove my face into my pillow and scream. Of course it can't be this easy. I'm four months too young to get a simple pill that can prevent pregnancy. Now I have to go down to the clinic and see a doctor. What if they ask me questions about what happened? I don't know if I can do this, but I can't risk becoming pregnant. What choice do I have?

My phone vibrates. I have a text message. I swipe the screen and poke the little green smiley face icon. My heart sinks when I see his name.

BRAD: What's up?

I look at the phone, confused. " 'What's up?' " How do I respond to this? Do I respond at all? I don't know what to say, so I don't reply. A few minutes later, I receive another text.

BRAD: I have practice until one if you want to come by. We can hang out later.

Is this a joke? Is he texting me by mistake? This message

has got to be for someone else. He's texting me like he didn't do anything wrong. He does realize he did something wrong. Doesn't he? I didn't imagine it all. Did I?

I feel myself being pulled into the past, into a memory I don't want to possess …

℃℥

Brad Swisher is the biggest boy on the football team. I look like a doll next to him. He's so cute and funny. I feel so lucky to get his attention at all. He's always so nice and polite. I am ecstatic when he asks me out.

On our first and only date, he takes me to the movies in his awesome red Camaro. We hold hands and kiss. Kissing is nice. We go back to his house. His parents are out. He shows me the refrigerator in the garage where his dad keeps the beer. He takes a bottle, offering me one, but I decline.

I've tasted beer before and I don't like it. He seems to guzzle the first bottle down too fast. I notice, but I don't say anything. I don't see how people can handle the nasty after-taste beer leaves in your mouth. I don't want to ruin our first date by pointing out how unhealthy and unattractive it is to guzzle down nasty beer one right after the other, so I stay quiet about it. He tosses the first bottle. Grabs another.

"Are you sure you don't want one?"

"I don't like beer. Do you have soda?"

"Yeah." He pulls a can of Coke out of the fridge. "Want some rum with that?"

I laugh uneasily. "Just straight up Coke is fine."

"Don't tell me you don't drink."

"I do," I lie. "I just don't feel like drinking now. Maybe next time."

He puts his arm around me, and we go inside. "Let me show you my room."

I'm excited that I get to see the inside of his house. Here I am in Brad Swisher's house. I can't wait to text Cassie. Tell her about this. He gives me the grand tour of the house that ends at his bedroom. I hover in his doorway, suddenly uneasy. Hold my Coke with both hands.

His room is a typical boy's room. Messy sheets on his bed. Clothes strewn over the floor. Everything is messy except for his football gear, which is neatly arranged on his dresser next to a shelf of trophies. He points to each trophy and gives me the details on when, where, how, and why he won each one. I smile, pretending to be interested. I'm not into sports, but I don't want him knowing that because he's the one I'm into.

Yes, he talks too much, but that's okay. There is just something about him that drives me crazy. I can't put my finger on it, but I love watching him and listening to him talk. He has such a magnetic personality. Everyone at school seems to like him. He has a way of making me feel special, like the luckiest girl in the world.

"Wow, you're so lucky to have so many trophies." I say,

just trying to make small talk. Show interest in something he cares about.

He finishes his beer. Walks up to me. He smiles, looking down at me. "Nah, I'm lucky to have you."

He leans down and pecks me on the lips. He tastes like beer, but I don't mind. My stomach is full of butterflies. All I can think is he kissed me! I can't wait to tell Cassie! I don't want this night to end. When I look at the clock, it's almost seven. Mom will be home soon. She doesn't know I went out on a date this afternoon.

"I hate to do this, but you have to take me home now."

"You never told your mom about me?"

I shake my head.

"Hey, it's okay. Let me grab another beer and I'll drive you home."

He gets me home with an hour to spare. He walks me up to my door and kisses me. I'm no expert at kissing, but he's fantastic! Even with the nasty aftertaste of beer, I don't want him to stop.

"Can I come in and use your bathroom?"

"Um, yeah sure."

I show him to the bathroom. "It's there. I'm going to run upstairs and put my phone on the charger. I'll be right back."

Before I put it on the charger, I sneak in a quick text to Cassie.

ME: OMG! Brad is in my house! TTYL

When I turn around, Brad is in my doorway.

"That was quick," I say in a little startled squeak.

He comes in and looks around my room. "Well, I showed you mine. I want to see yours."

"Oh. Well, here it is. Not much to see, though."

He walks up to me and puts his hands on my waist and pulls me close. "There's plenty to see. We still have time before your mom comes home."

"Time for what?"

"Get on the bed."

I draw back and look at him. He smiles and pushes me toward the bed. He's trying to be playful, but the feeling creeping up my spine is nowhere near playful.

"No," I say. "You need to go now. My mom will be home soon."

"I'll sneak out the window." He pushes me down onto the bed. "Kiss me."

Before I can reply, he shoves his tongue into my mouth. I'm trying to disconnect my face from his mouth and squirm out from under him. But his body gets heavier each time I move.

At some point I manage to disconnect my face long enough to speak. "Brad, get off me!"

"Come on, Peyton." His breath is warm and sour with beer as he kisses me. His hands are feeling me up. "You're so hot."

My awesome night is quickly turning into a nightmare. The safety I once felt with him rapidly turns into fear. I've never prayed so hard in my life for Mom to come walking through the door.

When he starts drifting underneath my clothes, I grab at his hands and push them off me. Each time I push his hands away from one part of my body, they quickly land somewhere else they don't belong. He's like wrestling an octopus.

"Get off me!" His weight is crushing me. I can barely breathe. "Stop!"

He tries putting his hand up my shirt. I say no, I'm not ready for that. I pull one hand down. The other one goes up my shirt. I pull both hands down. Both hands are unbuttoning my jeans. He's still kissing me, pressing into me. I can't keep up with his hands.

"Relax," he says. "Let me do it."

"No. I don't want to."

"Of course you do." He jerks my pants down. "It will feel good. Trust me."

"My mom will be home soon. I can't." I'm pulling my pants up. He pulls up my shirt. "Brad, stop."

"Shhh. It's okay."

His mouth is all over me. I'm squirming, trying to get out from under his weight. I pull my shirt down. He grabs my pants again and pulls them off before I can stop him.

I tighten my thighs together as he kisses my belly. He wedges one hand between my legs.

"I don't want to do this."

"A hot girl like you? I know you've done it before."

"No, I haven't." I'm pushing his head off me as he goes down farther. "I don't like this! Get off me!"

He slides up to me. Shoves his tongue into my mouth. This isn't kissing. I feel like he's trying to swallow my face. I can't talk with his tongue down my throat. I'm pushing at him with both hands. I feel his hand still forcing its way between my thighs. I'm squeezing them harder, but he's too strong.

"Come on, let me in."

"Stop!"

My thighs give way. There's a searing pain between my legs that goes into my stomach.

CHAPTER 4

Cassie calls, but I let it go to voice mail. I don't want to talk. Then she texts me.

CASSIE: Girl, where you at? Your man is here looking for you.

My man? Suddenly Brad and I are an item after one date? I haven't talked to her since yesterday. I don't know what to say to her. She's my best friend. I tell her everything. But not this. I can't tell her this.

ME: Mom has me helping her around the house.

CASSIE: Call me later and tell me all about last night.

ME: Okay.

Not okay, but I don't know what to say to her. I don't know what to do. I have to get out of my room, out of my house and think. I just need time alone to think. I grab my jacket and my phone. I really don't want my phone, but I can't risk leaving it here for Mom to see.

I go for a walk down by the river. It's quiet here. No one will bother me. I will be able to think.

In warmer weather the park would be full of boats, water-skiers, and fishermen. People would be having cookouts and picnics. They would be playing with their kids or walking their dogs. But it's barely forty degrees. The park is pretty empty.

An elderly couple is sitting on a nearby bench. A flock of seagulls hovers overhead. The couple is tossing popcorn into the flock. Every now and then a brave one will swoop in and grab a piece off the ground. The birds bicker over a piece of popcorn. Steal from one another. I like feeding the birds. Especially at this bench where a sign reads Do Not Feed the Wildlife. Ironic, huh?

A barge moves through the water. Its wake washes clams onto the shore. I walk close enough to collect the live clams. Toss them back into the water. I call it clam skipping. It's like rock skipping, but with clams. I make a sport out of it, but at the same time I'm saving them from certain death.

Every now and then I stumble on a dead fish. Usually a catfish or walleye. I always wonder how they wash up onshore and die in the sun. The biggest fish I find is at least two-feet long. It would have made a great catch for a lucky fisherman. Maybe even a good meal. What a waste.

The air is colder by the water. I wish I wore a heavier jacket. Still I walk, stepping over a dead fish, skipping another clam, and inhaling the fresh chilly air. I cross a boat launch and make my way to the bike trail. From here I can walk into town.

I walk down the trail. It leads to a bridge that crosses the river into town. On the other side of the bridge is the police station. I find myself standing outside it. Just standing there, staring at the front door. Watching people go in and come out. I have never been inside the police station before. I wonder if it looks like it does on the TV shows.

"Are you okay, miss?"

Startled, I turn to a uniformed police officer.

"Can I help you?" he asks.

I can feel my mouth moving. No words are coming out, though. It's like I forgot how to speak. He reaches out and touches my arm. "Are you okay?"

Physical contact makes me flinch. I take a step back. "I'm okay."

I glance around, hoping nobody I know has seen me in front of the police station. Talking to a cop no less. What if Brad sees me? Paranoia sets in. He can't see me. He will think I am reporting him. What will he do?

I hurry away from the officer without looking back. After I cross the street, I slow my pace. Main Street is busy on this chilly Saturday morning. People are walking around from shop to shop. It's been a hard winter. Although it's barely spring, people are taking advantage of the nicer weather.

I see my gym teacher carrying a bag out of a restaurant.

I turn and walk the opposite direction, away from her. A block down and around the corner, I see some girls from school coming out of the candy store. The bad thing about living in a small town is that you always run into somebody you know. I turn away and step into the pet store. I browse the wall of dog leashes long enough for the girls to walk past the window.

I continue walking through town until I come to a long brick building. It's the town's public health clinic. This is a free clinic for people who don't have much money. I've heard that teenagers can come here and get free birth control without any questions asked. This is one place I never imagined I would be. I have good health insurance under Mom. But I can't use it without her coming with me.

The parking lot is full of cars. A woman walks out the door with a baby in a carrier. Two small children follow her. I look around, afraid someone I know will see me standing here. What if I see someone I know inside? That terrifies me. But what choice do I have? What's worse? Being embarrassed or being pregnant?

I lower my head. Pull the door open quickly. Duck inside before anyone can see me. A short hallway opens up to a large waiting area. There are rows of multi-colored chairs.

I quickly scan the room as I walk up to the counter and stand in line. There are three people ahead of me. Only two people working the front counter. Each person gets called up one at a time. When it's my turn, I go up to the counter and speak with a middle-aged Hispanic woman.

"Good morning." She smiles.

"Hi." It's hard to make eye contact because I'm so ashamed. "I need help with"—I lower my voice to almost a whisper—"pregnancy."

"Okay." She shuffles through some papers. Hands me a clipboard and a pen. "Fill these out. Bring them back up to the counter when you're done."

I take the clipboard. Find a seat as far away from everyone as possible.

I fill out the papers as best I can. Then I stand in line again. I return the clipboard to the same woman. She briefly looks over the documents.

"Take a seat. Someone will call your name."

I return to my seat in the back row. Check out the back of everyone's head. Wonder what their stories are. Why are they here? One woman is consoling her crying baby. Small children bounce restlessly around. Play with toys. If all of these people are ahead of me, then I'm in for a long wait.

I see a girl from school come through the door. Tammy Davison. She's the pregnant girl at school. Her belly is so big. She looks like she's hiding a basketball under her shirt. I've never talked to her before. She's just a girl I see around all the time. I've never even said hi to her. But I've heard the gossip.

Kids talk about her. How she's had sex with some football players at our school. She's known for being easy. A cheap date.

I've heard boys say that she will have sex with anyone for a beer. They also say she has crabs and doesn't bathe. They laugh about the skid marks in her underwear. I've always wondered … if she's supposed to be so gross, why have so many boys claimed to have "hit that"?

I've heard Brad talk about her to other boys. About how nasty she is. How he would never touch someone like her. Some of those boys can be so cruel. I would die if they talked about me like they talk about her.

Almost two hours pass when it's my turn. A woman in pink scrubs steps out of a door. Calls off a few names. Mine is one of them. I think about not going. Why not just sit here? Pretend I don't hear my name. Then I can make a run for the door. But I know I have to do what I came here to do, no matter how unpleasant it is.

I go through the door with the other people. Each of us is placed in separate rooms.

There's an exam table. It's covered in white paper and a folded gown.

"Put on the gown. The doctor will be with you soon."

I see the gown. "But—" I turn as she closes the door.

I don't know why I have to change into a gown when I'm only here to talk to the doctor. I'm only here for a pill.

Why would the doctor want to examine me first? I'm not mentally prepared to get undressed for an exam.

Still, I change into the gown, hoping that it's unnecessary. I just want to get this done fast. Get it over with. I fold my clothes on the chair. Sit on the edge of the exam table. I drape a paper blanket across my legs because the gown gapes when I sit down. The paper blanket is so small, I may as well cover myself with a paper towel.

There isn't a clock in the room. I have no idea how long I'm waiting. At one point I think they forgot about me. Should I get dressed and leave? I can figure something else out, right? Then there's a knock on the door.

The door opens. Another woman in pink scrubs enters. A tall dark-skinned man in a white lab coat follows her. When I realize the doctor is a man, I freak a little. I've always had a female doctor. I've never even talked to a male doctor before.

The nurse closes the door. She's holding a clipboard. The doctor smiles. Extends his hand to me. I look at it. He wants to shake my hand. My hand is shaking as I clasp his hand in mine and briefly shake it.

"I'm Dr. Cho. Are you Peyton?"

I nod. His disposition is friendly. But I find myself wanting to run out of the room, gown or not.

"What brings you here today, Peyton?"

I have to fight the urge to run away and get down to

business. I need to tell him the facts. No over explaining of anything. Just the facts.

"I tried to get Plan B today. But they wouldn't give it to me because I'm not seventeen."

"When did you have unprotected sex?"

"Last night."

"Are you on any birth control?"

"No. It was my first time."

The nurse hands him the clipboard. I assume it has the papers I filled out. He takes a moment to read through it.

"Have you ever seen a gynecologist before?"

I shake my head no.

"Normally young ladies should begin getting a yearly exam once menstruation begins. First let me give you a pelvic exam. Then we can talk about birth control. Okay?"

No, this is not okay. Totally not okay. But do I have a choice at this point? I can't back out now. I've come this far.

He instructs me to lie back. Tells me to scoot my bottom to the edge of the exam table. He pulls out two metal attachments. Calls them stirrups. He guides my feet to rest in them. I stare at the ceiling.

"I need you to relax," he says in a soothing voice. "Let your knees fall apart. Relax."

I'm trying to force myself to relax. My muscles are fighting it. My legs won't stop shaking. I take a deep breath. Stare intently at the white ceiling. My heart is beating hard in my chest. I focus on my heartbeat and on my breath.

"What grade are you in?"

"What? Oh, I'm a junior."

"Eastlake Community High School?"

Why is he asking me these questions? I hear him clinking around with the instruments on the tray—things that I'm afraid to look at. His voice is so calm and soothing. But when he touches my legs, I tense up.

"Yeah," I say.

"My daughter is a senior there," he says. "Okay, Peyton. Relax your legs for me. I'm going to insert a speculum to help me examine you. This might be a little uncomfortable."

I feel this cold metal push inside me and open me up. I gasp. I'm so sore. I notice the water stains on the ceiling, the different shades and textures. There's a spider crawling across the ceiling too. I hate spiders. I hope it doesn't fall on me.

"I'm going to use a cotton swab on your cervix. It won't hurt."

I focus on the spider. The sensation caused by the swab is weird. It doesn't hurt. I'm focusing on my heartbeat, my breath, and staying relaxed. Praying he will hurry and take that thing out of me. Then there is a noise. I feel myself close up as he slides out the cold metal.

"All done. That wasn't so bad, was it?"

Yes, yes it was.

"No."

"Was this your first time having sex?"

"Yes."

"Was this your boyfriend?"

"No." Why did I say that? I shouldn't have said that.

He stands up next to me. Lifts my gown. Presses on my belly. It hurts. I'm trying not to make eye contact with him. But I can see him looking at me, maybe watching the expressions of pain on my face. I'm staring hard at that little spider. It's fumbling around in its web on the ceiling. Don't fall on me, little spider. Do not—

"Was the sex consensual?

"What do you mean?"

"Did you want to have sex?"

I hesitate. How do I answer this? This should be a simple yes or no answer, but it's not that simple. I realize I'm taking too long to answer. Does he know? Can he tell by examining me that the sex was forced?

"It was just sex."

"Peyton, I want you to relax and take a deep breath." With one hand on my belly, he slips his other hand between my legs. He slides his fingers in, pressing around.

"Stop! I don't like this." My hands are gripping the

table now. I'm suddenly cast back to last night when Brad was on top of me. His hands everywhere. Touching me. Groping me.

"This is part of the exam, Peyton. Does this hurt?"

"Yes. I don't like it. Stop touching me."

I'm shaking my hands in the air. I feel almost hysterical. Then he pulls his fingers out. Lowers my gown. Takes my feet out of the stirrups. Takes my hand. Helps me to sit up.

"It's okay. Breathe." He's holding my hands. "You're okay."

I can feel myself shaking. I force myself to look at him so I can show myself this is a doctor—it's not Brad. I notice the look he shares with the nurse. She hands him the clipboard again. He writes something down.

"I will give you the Plan B pill. It's one pill. Take it with a full glass of water. There should be little to no side effects. Come back to see me in two weeks. We will do a pregnancy test to make sure it did what it's supposed to do. I'm also going to give you some information. It's to see a counselor. For free. It's also confidential."

I nod. I think he knows what I'm not telling him. Why would he want me to see a counselor if he doesn't know? All I care about is the pill. Just give me the damn pill and let me go. I want to go home.

"It was nice meeting you, Peyton. You can get dressed

now. Wait here and the nurse will come back with your medication and your release papers."

After they leave the room, I get dressed as quickly as I can. The comfort of my own clothes makes me feel safe again. I sit on the exam table and wait for the nurse to return. She walks in. Holds a pill cup with a single white pill. There's a cup of water. I went through all of this embarrassment for that one little white pill. I pop it into my mouth. Finish off the cup of water. There, it's done. Problem solved. I can move on now, right?

გ

That afternoon I come home. I can hear Mom vacuuming upstairs. I hear the rumbling of the washer and dryer in the utility room off the kitchen. Immediately I think of my bed sheets. The vacuum stops. Mom comes downstairs. She has that look on her face. She's mad about something.

"Come here," she says. I follow her to the utility room where my hamper is sitting next to the washer. She fishes through the hamper and pulls out my sheets, marked red with blood. "This isn't something you throw into the hamper. You should have soaked them first."

My mouth drops open, but no words come out.

"We are both women. You don't have to be embarrassed when you get your period. We can talk about these things. Okay?"

I nod dumbly.

She tosses the sheets back into the hamper. "These were nice sheets. Now they're probably stained."

My eyes hurt. She thinks its blood from my period. Can't she tell it's not menstrual blood? Once again I find myself wanting to cry, but I can't. "I'm sorry." I hurry up to my room.

"It's nothing to cry over, Peyton," she calls after me.

I think a small part of me wants her to find out. I'm disappointed that she doesn't know. Aren't mothers supposed to know these things? I feel like I have this huge secret that will make me explode if I don't tell someone. It makes me angry that Mom doesn't have the sixth sense enough to know.

Cassie calls me. This time I answer.

"Are you still busy with your mom?"

"Yeah, kinda. Actually, I think I'm grounded."

"What did you do?"

I don't know how to answer this.

"What's wrong? Something's wrong."

I know if I talk to her, she will know something is wrong. Now what do I do? Tell her the truth or a lie?

"I just can't talk right now. I'll call you tomorrow." I hang up.

CHAPTER 5

I wake up the next morning and just lie there. It's almost ten o'clock. I have no reason to get out of bed. My body is exhausted. My mind is exhausted. I feel as if I just woke up from the longest bad dream ever.

My stomach rumbles. I realize I'm hungry. When did I eat last? Friday. When I ate pizza before the movie, which I later puked up. Then there's the food I spit out Friday night. Does that even count? I listen to my rumbling belly as it cries out for food. I can't bring myself to eat.

I get dressed. Go downstairs. Mom asks me what I want for breakfast. My belly screams, give me everything! But I say I'm not hungry. I can't even think about putting in the effort to chew food. Swallow it. It's too much work.

I feel like I'm walking around with a wet blanket over me. Why can't Mom see it? I get angry with her because she can't see it. When I was little, she used to know everything. When I did something bad, she always knew. It didn't matter how much I would try to hide it from her.

How sneaky I thought I was being. So why the hell doesn't she know something's up?

I look at her across the room. Give her a dirty look. She doesn't see it. I should leave. Before she sees it and questions me about it.

I go upstairs to my room. Find the counseling brochure I got from the clinic. I read through it. The clinic offers free counseling and a 24/7 crisis hotline number to call. I don't need counseling. I just need enough time to pass. Then I'll forget about everything.

I just need time.

I'm not in crisis. I'm not suicidal or anything. I don't need to call the hotline. Who needs this information? Not me. But I can't bring myself to throw it away. Instead, I stuff it under my mattress along with my release papers from the clinic.

My phone vibrates. I just stare at it. What if it's him? I'm afraid to look at it. Is it another text that I won't respond to? I can avoid his texts but I can't avoid him. I'll have to face him tomorrow in school.

I can't avoid it.

I touch my phone. Open the screen. I'm relieved when I see Cassie's name.

CASSIE: How you doing?

ME: I'm okay. What's up?

CASSIE: Wanna hang out today?

I don't want to see anyone today.

ME: Not today. I don't feel well.

CASSIE: What's wrong?

ME: I'm just sick.

Several minutes pass. I think I'm in the clear.

CASSIE: I'm coming over.

I throw my phone down. Sometimes there is just no getting rid of that girl. I don't want to see anyone today. I just want to stay under my blanket where no one can hurt me.

An hour later, my door opens and Cassie comes in. She shuts the door behind her. Sits down on my bed. I sit up to face her.

"You look like crap."

"Yeah, I know."

"Maybe if you tell me about your date with Brad, you'll feel better."

She means to tease me. But I don't give her the reaction she's expecting. She notices this and her expression changes. I can't look her in the eyes. But she's looking at me, trying to figure me out. Cassie is my best friend. Normally I can tell her everything. But nothing about this is normal.

"Did something happen?"

I can feel her watching me. My mind goes blank as I desperately try to come up with a suitable lie.

"Peyton? Did he do something to you?"

I can't think. Can't look at her. I start shaking my

head, still trying to come up with an excuse. Why is it so hard to tell her the truth? Would telling her the truth be so bad? She's my best friend. She's always been there for me through thick and thin. I've always been able to trust her.

"If I tell you something, you have to promise me you won't tell anyone." I look her in the eyes now. "Promise me, Cassie."

"Okay, I promise."

ଔ

I know I should feel some relief that I told Cassie. I'm not alone in this anymore. I should feel some weight lifted off me. But I don't. Cassie wouldn't look at me at first. She looks everywhere but at me. Her mouth is working, as if she wants to say something, but nothing comes out.

Now that she knows, I feel dirty all over again. I feel the need to shower and scrub myself with bleach. I start scratching at my arms, as if I can scratch the filth off me.

I want her to say something. What is she thinking? Feeling? Some clue to help us move past this awkward silence. My phone vibrates on the table. I pick it up and look at it. It's another text message.

BRAD: Babe, are you mad at me? Why won't you text me back?

"Is that him?" Cassie is a sudden ball of fury, ready to release her rage. "Gimme that phone. I'm gonna kill him."

"I haven't talked to him. I don't know what to say."

"I'll talk to him. Gimme your phone."

"No, Cassie." I put it in my pocket. It's out of her reach.

"What are you gonna do when you see him at school tomorrow?"

I have no idea.

"If my brother finds out what he did to you, he'll kill him."

"You promised me you wouldn't tell anyone."

"But he can't get away with this."

"I don't want to cause any trouble."

"Peyton, this is not your fault. He's the one that started the trouble, not you."

I'm not sure about that. Some of this *has* to be my fault. I let him into my house, into my room. I could have screamed or fought harder or been more aggressive. There had to be something I could have done to stop it. But no matter how many times I go over it in my head …

So why do I feel like some of this is my fault?

If he were arrested, it would be my fault. If he were kicked off the football team, it would be my fault. If he were expelled from school, it would be my fault. Wouldn't it?

"I just … want to pretend like nothing ever happened."

"Peyton—"

"It's done! It's over. There's nothing I can do about it now."

Whether or not that's true, I just want to forget about it. Make it go away.

"Can I at least tell my brother to beat him up?"

I smile at the thought. Leave it to Cassie to make me smile, if only a little. We hang out for a few hours. Then Cassie goes home. She makes me feel almost normal again. She doesn't look at me differently or talk to me differently. She's my best friend in the whole world. She proved it to me today.

Honestly, telling her made me feel a little better. A weight has been lifted off my shoulders. Even with the relief comes the fear that Cassie may tell someone. She promised me she wouldn't. But still ...

CHAPTER 6

I walk into school. It's Monday. I feel like a different person. I keep my head down. I feel like if I make eye contact with anyone, they'll know I'm different. They'll know the hell my body went through. Who did it? They'll know I was at the clinic. I keep my head down because maybe someone saw me there. I don't want anyone to stop me. Ask me why I was at the clinic. I see Tammy Davison on the way to my locker. Quicken my pace to pass her.

I get to my locker. My brain fogs when I try to remember my combination. My hands are a little shaky. I know it's because I haven't eaten in a couple days. When I finally get my locker open, I just stand there. It's messy. Full of books and old assignments. I'm not thinking of anything in particular. I'm just standing there, looking inside.

I'm here. I can do this.

Then from behind me I feel hands on my waist. I freeze. Arms slide around me. A hard body presses against me. I catch my breath. A voice whispers in my ear.

"I got you now," he says. "Why haven't you returned my texts?"

I have to remind myself to breathe. I'm stiff. I can't move. I don't know what to say. His breath is hot against my skin as he kisses my ear. It makes me remember the smell of beer on his breath. How he shoved his tongue into my mouth.

"What's wrong, babe?"

I don't know what to say. How to react. I don't want to turn around. Don't want to face him. Don't want to make eye contact. I close my eyes.

What do I do?

"Uh-uh, no. Get your hands off my girl."

A familiar voice sends a wave of relief through me. I look over. Cassie and her brother, Shane, are walking toward us. At this point I'm not sure if this is a good thing or a bad thing. Brad releases me. I hold on to the locker door for support.

"What's up, Cassie?" Brad asks.

"You need to go," she tells him.

I'm looking at her, but she's locked her eyes on him. I can't look at Brad. I can only look at his arm. He's wearing his football letterman jacket. The white vinyl sleeve is more nonthreatening than eye contact.

"Come on, bro," Shane says. "Let them do their thing."

"What? I can't say hi to my girl?" Brad asks.

"She's not your girl," Cassie says.

"Feel free to step in here anytime, Peyton," Brad says. He nudges me playfully.

I can't look at him. I don't want to be in this situation. Don't want to confront him at school, or at all for that matter. I just want to forget about everything and hide.

"I need to talk to Cassie," I say. I refuse to look anyone in the eye. I just want them all to go away.

He puts his arms around me, then grabs my ass. I clench the locker door so tightly my fingernail splits to the skin. He walks away with Shane. Cassie watches them as they leave. When she puts her hand on my shoulder, I flinch.

"You okay?"

"Yeah." No, no I'm not.

"Did you say anything to him?"

"I couldn't. I just froze."

"You need to say something. He should be in jail for what he did."

"I know." She's right and I know it. "I just ... don't know."

"Peyton—"

"Cassie, I can't deal with this right now." I fumble through my locker, picking out books. My eyes sting from the tears. My vision is blurry.

"And what happens when you see him in class?"

I close my eyes. Bite my lip. I can't look at her. I don't want to deal with this. I don't want to be here. I want to drop everything. Run away. Go somewhere and be alone.

"I'll deal with it later," I say.

"I know you, Peyton," she huffs. "You're going to let that boy walk away. He's gonna do the same thing to another girl."

If he hasn't already …

"Please don't say anything, Cassie. I can't deal with this right now."

"There will never be a good time to deal with this."

She's right, but I don't know what else I can say. I just want her to leave it alone. Never mention it again. I regret telling her everything. How can I forget about this? How can I put it all behind me? Not when she wants me to confront him about it.

"Fine." She turns. Walks away.

I watch her leave. Down the hall I can see Brad and Shane. I see Cassie go up to Brad. Grab his arm. My heart thuds hard in my chest in anticipation. I can't hear what's being said, but I can see Cassie's face. Her hands move wildly. Her mouth is a hard line. She's telling him off.

Stop talking, Cassie, please stop talking! I'm begging her in my head.

I can't hear what she's saying. But I can see the

expressions on their faces. My mind assumes the worst. Shane takes a step back. Looks back and forth between his sister and his friend.

My heart thuds hard again. I can tell by the expression on his face. She told him. Shane looks at me. I can feel my eyes burn with salty tears.

Brad turns. Looks at me. My heart thuds hard again. He knows. A warm sensation drops from my chest into my stomach. I clutch my books to my chest. He starts walking toward me. I'm scared but I can't move.

She told him! I'm not ready for this. She promised me. Why did she do this? I can't believe she did this.

"What the hell, Peyton? Why are you talking trash about me?" He presses his body against me, pushing me into the lockers. "You told her I raped you?"

He says it so loud, the noise in the hall drops. I can feel people watching us.

Cassie pulls him away. Steps between him and me. "Back off."

"I want her to tell me." He gets in Cassie's face.

Shane grabs him by his shoulder and pulls him away. "Back off, bro."

Brad takes a step back. "Are you buying this garbage, bro?"

"Don't be stepping up on my sister like that."

STICKS AND STONES

"I'm trying to talk to the bitch behind her."

"Oh, I don't think so!" Cassie steps up to him. Shane pushes her back.

"Chill out," he tells her. "C'mon, bro. Let's get out of here."

"I'll"—he's so angry his nostrils are flaring—"deal with you later." Then he walks away.

I can feel people watching us. I can't believe this is happening. Shane lingers behind. Looks at me. I can't meet his eyes. "Is it true?"

My mouth is open, but no words come out. I look at Cassie. Her good intentions have become the ultimate betrayal. I can't look at either of them. I can feel eyes on me. I can hear words being mumbled in the hall. But I can't lift my eyes from the floor. I feel beaten and defeated. Gripping my books to my chest, I run down the hall to my first class.

ങ

Mrs. Fey explains the Pythagorean theorem. The kind of math that requires full brain function. I have none. I can hear the words. But nothing makes sense. I stare at my open textbook. Replay the incident in the hall in my mind. Over and over and over and over …

What could I have done to prevent this?

Why couldn't I have been stronger?

Why am I such a coward?

I couldn't talk. Couldn't respond. All I did was run away like a fraidycat. Is this what I've become?

Mrs. Fey is rambling on about numbers as her chalk scratches marks onto the blackboard. The sound is so irritating. Clicking on the board. Speaking in numbers that make no sense. Clicking of chalk with numbers, letters, explanations.

Clicking.

Clicking.

Clicking.

I stuff my book into my bag. Hurry toward the door. Mrs. Fey stops. Says something to me. I don't know what she says. Kids mumble. I refuse to make eye contact with anyone. I stare at the door and just keep going. I don't respond to my name. I don't look back. I just keep going down the hall. I don't stop until I'm through the front doors. Hit fresh air.

I'm on autopilot. Breathe in. Breathe out. Breathe in. I'm down to the street before I realize it. I don't know where I'm going. I'm just walking. Getting away from the school. I need to clear my mind.

I walk down to the football field. Sit on the bleachers in the first row. No classes will be using the field until second period. I have a little time to myself. I feel so betrayed. Cassie promised she wouldn't say anything. But she did! I didn't want anyone to know. I didn't want to make it real. I just want to forget about it. Make it go away. I can't forget about it if everyone knows about it. It won't go away if everyone's talking about it. How can she betray me like this?

I feel so lost. So alone.

I'm sure I'll be in trouble for walking out of class. I'm sure Mrs. Fey will want to know why I left. She may even give me a referral. Send me to the office. What do I say? I can tell her I had to throw up. That should work.

I know I need to go back into school. If I don't, they will call Mom. She'll want to know what happened. I look at the time on my phone. First period is half over. I'll go in. Be on time to my second class. Pretend as if nothing happened. If that doesn't work, I'll throw up on my desk. Call it a day. Right now I think I can throw up on demand.

CHAPTER 7

In my next class I take a seat in the back of the room. I open my book. Pretend to study. Avoid looking at anyone. Cassie comes in and quietly takes a seat next to me. She's in most of my classes. We always sit together. I'm surprised she's still sitting next to me after what happened. Does she even know I'm mad at her? I think it's obvious.

I ignore her.

I pretend not to notice when Brad walks in. But in a perfectly awkward moment, we briefly make eye contact. He sits a few rows ahead of me, next to Desi, the head cheerleader. They lean in together for a moment. Then Desi looks back at me.

I pretend to read my textbook. It's no secret Desi has always liked him. It's no secret she has always hated me. She hates anyone who isn't popular. Anyone who has something—or someone—she wants.

Think about it. The head cheerleader and the star

quarterback, they are destined to be together. So why was he interested in me in the first place?

After class I make sure I'm the last one to leave. I see Cassie hanging back, as if she's waiting for me to catch up. Then she gives up and leaves. When I walk into the hall, Brad is waiting for me.

"We need to talk." He walks along with me. I stare straight ahead without stopping.

"Stop ignoring me. Talk to me."

He grabs me. Pushes me up against some lockers. A few kids scatter, but no one intervenes. I look around, hoping someone will help me. Hoping Cassie is nearby to step in again. He steps up against me, looking down at me. Then he pushes all of his weight into me. If he wants to make me feel small? Mission accomplished.

"Why did you say that crap about me?"

I try to push him away. But he pushes into me even more.

"You know what you did was wrong," I say. "Get off me!"

"Know what, Peyton?" He leans down. Speaks in a low voice so only I can hear him. "Bitches like you are a dime a dozen. You're nothing but a dirty whore."

I don't know how to respond to this. I feel as if he physically crushed me. I have never felt so small and worthless in my life. This isn't the boy I fell head over heels for. Who is this person?

He punches the locker next to me. Then storms off, leaving me cowering and afraid to move.

I skip lunch and go to the library. It's quiet and nearly empty. No one will bother me here. I stop at the desk. Take a piece of tape from the dispenser. Wrap it around my broken fingernail. It's been annoying me all morning.

I sit down at one of the wooden tables. Pull out my English book. I have every intention of reading chapter eleven for the test, but I just stare at it instead. I can't focus on the words. I'm so scatterbrained. All I can think about is how small and worthless Brad makes me feel.

I go over it in my head. The look in his eyes. The words he said. His anger toward me.

He makes me feel as if *I* did something wrong. I feel like this is my fault. If only I kept my mouth shut and didn't tell Cassie, none of this would have happened. I could have just …

Just what?

Again I relive that night in my head. How many beers did he have? Should I blame the beer? How many times did I say no? Did I say it enough? Did I say it loud enough so he could hear me? I tried to push him off. Did I try hard enough?

I get this queasy feeling. It's deep in the pit of my stomach. A sickness of shame and guilt makes me want to puke. I was a virgin. I didn't want to lose my virginity this way. And *he's* mad at me?

The bell rings. Time for my next class.

Ignoring Cassie is hard. She still sits next to me in almost every class. Lingers behind after class, as if she's waiting for me to look up and smile at her. Pretend like everything is okay. It's too exhausting pretending like everything is okay.

It's exhausting ignoring my best friend and hating myself for it. Yet I continue with this crazy behavior all afternoon. Until I don't even know why anymore.

I pretend not to notice the dirty looks from Brad and his friends. I pretend not to hear my name. The humiliating comments from Desi and her crew.

I look at the clock. I need food. Something to eat. But the thought of putting something into my mouth nauseates me. Chewing. Swallowing. I just can't do it.

As soon as the last bell rings, my ass is out the door.

 os

When I get home, I go to the bathroom. Get a bandage to replace the tape on my finger. Splitting my nail to the skin really hurts. I wrap the tip of my finger to secure the nail. I know it will come off eventually, but I don't have the nerve to pull it off. Finish the job myself. Once my nail is secure, I realize how distracting it was. The distraction was a relief.

I look in the mirror above the sink. Stare at my reflection. I look older. My face appears thin. Pale. I look broken.

I'm a fragile shell of the person I used to be three days ago. Does anyone notice?

I grab a glass. Fill it up with water. Take a sip. I watch myself in the mirror as I take a sip. My mouth is ugly. I look ugly sipping water out of a clear glass. Why did Brad want to kiss my ugly mouth? I look closer at my pudgy nose. I never noticed how large my pores are until now.

I examine my eyebrows, carefully plucked, but natural. I've never understood why girls wax off half their eyebrows, then draw them in again. The closer I look, the more hairy my brows appear. The closer I look at myself, the more hideous I appear. I never realized I was so ugly. Why would anyone want to date me? Or rape me, for that matter?

I put the glass on the sink. It falls. Shatters. Tears sting my eyes. My throat is closing as I fight the tears. Maybe crying will make me feel better.

No one is home.

No one will hear me.

No one will know.

I take in a hard breath. Let it all out. I allow myself a few minutes to cry. Every now and then I look at myself in the mirror. See how ugly I am when I cry. I start picking up the pieces of glass in the sink. There is a large piece. It fits perfectly in the palm of my hand.

I close my fingers around the broken shard, feeling it

cut into my hand. I catch my breath as the glass punctures holes in my skin. I stop crying.

The tighter I squeeze, the less pain I feel. The physical pain drowns out all of my mental anguish. Blood wells up between my fingers. Drips down into the sink.

There's so much blood.

Drip.

Drip.

Drip.

The sink is red with my blood. I open my hand. What does it look like? The glass is embedded into my palm in four different places. I pull it out, leaving four oozing holes. It doesn't hurt much, but my hand feels numb.

I grab a towel. Wrap my hand. It looks really bad. I don't know if the pressure will stop the bleeding. I think I need stitches.

I go up to my room. Look for the old Ace bandage I had when I sprained my wrist last summer. I find it and wrap my hand. I grab the paper with the crisis line number on it. Am I in crisis?

Should I call?

What would I say?

Would I call them just to tell them I cut my hand on purpose?

Would I say I cut myself because the physical pain is better than the mental pain?

What would they say?

I'm curious. I find my phone. Dial the number. I keep my finger over the button to end the call. Just in case.

"Crisis line, this is Lisa. How may I help you?"

I didn't expect someone to answer on the first ring. What should I say? Am I in crisis? Or do I just want someone to talk to?

"Hello? Is someone there?"

I hang up. Toss the phone aside.

The blood is soaking through the bandage. The queasy feeling in my stomach won't go away. I need a new bandage. Need to go to the hospital. Need to call Mom. Tell her I hurt myself. I should call her. I look at the phone and know I should call her.

But I can't. She will ask questions. I can't answer any questions. After everything that happened. After telling Cassie about Brad, I can't handle any more grief.

I search the cabinets for a first aid kit. Once I get the bleeding to stop, I wrap my hand in a thick layer of gauze. Tape it off. I take the blood-soaked towel and bandage, stuff them into the bottom of the trash can. Mom will never find them there.

CHAPTER 8

The next morning I wake up. My hand is throbbing. I unwrap it. See how red and swollen the cuts are. I go to the bathroom. Wash my hand with warm water and antibacterial soap.

It hurts.

I let my hand air dry as I go through the medicine cabinet. What will help ease the pain? I find an old prescription of painkillers. Mom hurt her back last year. I read the label. It expired a few months ago. Trying to open a childproof lid with one hand, I spill half the pills into the sink. I take two, then put the rest back.

I rewrap my hand. Get ready for school. Mom is in the car waiting for me. The pills kick in. I cover my hand with a jacket so Mom doesn't see. I get lightheaded and nauseated. Almost fall down the stairs.

"Are you okay?" Mom asks as I get into the car.

"Yeah, just tired."

She drops me off at school. Suddenly those steep steps leading up to the entrance seem impossible to climb. It takes all my focus to get to the top. I hold on to the rail to keep from falling down. I realize now that taking those pills on an empty stomach was a stupid thing to do.

I walk down the hall to my locker. I pass Cassie. She turns to look at me. I look away and keep moving. It feels weird avoiding her. I don't like it. I don't like this thick fog I'm moving through even more. Up ahead are Brad and a few of his friends. They're standing by his locker.

"Hey, bro, do you smell that?"

"Smells like skank."

"Oh, that's just Peyton."

I walk past as they all laugh at me.

It bothers me but I don't respond. I'm so numb from the painkillers. The fogginess is slowing me down. It distracts me enough that I don't see Desi and her friends coming down the hall. Next thing I know, one of them pushes me into the wall and keeps walking.

I make it to my locker. Get the books I need for my first two classes. My chest tightens. My heart starts beating fast, pounding hard in my chest. A splitting headache creeps up one side of my head. I feel like I'm getting lost. I have to close my eyes for a minute.

Just for a minute.

I lean my head against my locker for support. My books fall to the floor. I don't care. I just need to close my eyes … just for a minute.

୯୫

It takes me a moment to realize where I am. I don't know what time it is when I wake up. The light is dim. When I look out the window, the sky is a deep blue. The lights are on. I can't tell if it's sunset or sunrise.

I'm wearing a thin hospital gown. It freaks me out a little wondering how many people saw me naked when they changed me out of my clothes. Underneath my gown I have little sticky things all over my chest. These are attached to wires that connect me to a machine. I have an oxygen tube up my nose. There's an IV taped to the back of my good hand. My other hand is wrapped. It feels numb. There's a little clip at the tip of my index finger that's kind of annoying.

There are machines all around me. They have lights and digital numbers that I don't know how to read. I'm hooked up. There's a chair in the corner. Mom's sitting there. She's quietly snoring. I fumble around. Find a remote to raise the bed a little.

"Mom?" My throat hurts. My mouth is dry. "Mom?"

She stirs slightly. Rolls her head. Then she gets up and comes to my bedside. Takes a cup of ice from a little rolling table. I try taking the cup from her, but all the wires get in my way.

"I got it." She gives me a spoonful of ice chips to crunch on. "Is that better?"

I nod. It feels so good to have some moisture in my mouth.

"What happened?"

She explains everything to me. I passed out from a rapid heartbeat. They call it supraventricular tachycardia, or SVT for short.

Doctors gave me a shot that reset my heartbeat to a normal rhythm. If that's not freaky enough, my throat hurts because at some point they put a tube down it to help me breathe. I'm so glad I wasn't awake for any of that!

She tells me that I was also dehydrated. And I had a severe vitamin deficiency. I assume it's from not eating for days—but I don't tell her that.

The deep cuts on my hand didn't help either. There was still glass in my skin. I got a total of eight stitches for that. Plus a heavy dose of antibiotics. Then she explains the machines. What each one means. The bag of fluids to keep me hydrated. The oxygen to help me breathe. The heart monitor for all those little wires stickered to my chest. She spoon-feeds me ice chips as she calmly explains.

"You slept all day," she says.

"Still tired."

"Go back to sleep, then. I'm not going anywhere. I'll be right here."

She stays beside my bed, playing with my hair. Stroking my arm until I doze off.

CHAPTER 9

It seems like every time I get comfortable sleeping, a nurse comes in and wakes me. Takes my blood for tests. Takes my blood pressure. Fumbles around with all the wires and tubes. It's *so* annoying. They tell me to get some rest. But when I do, they wake me up.

By six in the morning a nurse gives me a menu. Explains to us how to order breakfast. I'm still not hungry. But the nurse says I have some pills I need to take. On a full stomach. Otherwise they'll make me sick.

I have to tell Mom to go to work. She wants to stay. I don't want her to stay. I want to be alone. So she calls her boss. Says she will be late. Stays with me for another hour to help me eat breakfast. She basically spoon-feeds me like a baby. Puts a straw in my soda. Holds it for me as I drink. When I'm done and ready for a nap, she leaves for work. Promises she'll be back later.

It's around noon. I'm lying in bed. Flipping through the TV channels. There's a knock on my door. A man's voice asks if he can come in. Thinking it's a male nurse, I tell him it's okay. My curtain moves aside. An older man in a black shirt, white collar, and knit sweater comes in. He smiles. Introduces himself.

"I'm Pastor Glenn. I notice you don't have a religion selected. Would you like to choose religious services?"

"I'm not religious, so probably not."

"Are you an atheist?"

"No, I just don't have a religion."

"That's okay. You don't have to be religious to talk to me." He seems nice. Easygoing. "If there's anything you would like to talk about, I would be happy to sit here. Listen."

His open invitation catches me off guard. I feel like I should make a confession. But I have nothing. Other than lying to Mom. Stealing money from her purse. Taking the car without her permission—but it's not like I killed anybody.

There's something about him that sets me at ease. Makes me want to talk to him. I don't know about what. I don't know why, but I don't want him to leave. It's been so long since I had a father figure in my life. I forgot what it feels like.

"You can sit down if you want."

He pulls up a chair next to my bed. "Have you had many visitors today?"

I shake my head. "My mom will come back when she gets off work."

"Would you like to talk about why you're here?"

Long story.

"I wouldn't know where to start."

"How about telling me how you hurt your hand?"

I look at my hand. It's all wrapped up. The stitches itch. My hand burns. I start telling him what happened. He sits down. Listens to me. The more he listens, the more I talk. I don't know why I keep talking. But I end up telling him everything.

"You're not going to tell anyone, are you?"

He shakes his head. "Not if you don't want me to."

"That's what my best friend said."

"From what you told me about her, she reacted out of love for you." He hands me his card. It has his contact information on it. "Try not to stay mad at her for too long. You may not see it now, but everything happens for a reason. Bad things happen to good people. Sometimes good things can come out of the bad."

I stare at his card, suddenly unable to make eye contact with him. "What good things can possibly come out of me being raped?"

I can feel him staring at me. But I refuse to look up and make eye contact with him. He's taking so long to answer me, I wonder if he even has an answer.

"I can help you if you let me, Peyton. I'll be praying for you."

❀

I leave the hospital that night. They have to wait for Mom. I have a prescription for antibiotics and Vicodin for the pain in my hand. I also have to take a multivitamin and potassium pills until I can start eating right.

I don't say anything to Mom about Pastor Glenn. I don't know why. Mom's not religious. At least not that I know of. We don't go to church. She never talks about religion. I don't even know what Mom's views are. I feel some comfort having Pastor Glenn as my secret friend.

CHAPTER 10

om wants to stay home from work with me. But I say no. Assure her I'll be fine. Although she doesn't admit it, I think she blames herself. She didn't notice what I did to my hand. Didn't realize I wasn't eating. Please go to work, I say. I want her gone. I just want to be alone.

Right after she leaves for work, I take a shower. Get ready for the day. Not because I have any real plans. After two days in a hospital gown, my own clothes feel good. I'm even feeling a little better. Probably because I'm eating. Taking vitamins. But I'm sure the pain pills are playing a major role too. I take a pain pill. Within minutes I'm flooded with a peaceful feeling.

I eat a banana. Potassium is good for my heart. I don't want to have a rapid heartbeat again. That was scary. The banana is delicious. Bananas are wonderful things. I love bananas, so I eat another. Yeah, I'm not feeling any pain now. I feel happy. I feel love. I feel—

The pill is making me high.

I find Pastor Glenn's card. Look it over. He's so nice. Such a great guy. His church is in walking distance. Down the street from the police station. I probably shouldn't leave the house until this painkiller wears off a little. But it's such a beautiful day outside. Life is just wonderful. I grab my purse and jacket. Go for a walk.

I take the long way into town, through the park. It's down by the river. The sun keeps me warm and comfortable even though it's cold. It's colder by the river. But someone is brave enough to take their boat out onto the water. Some garbage and driftwood washes onto the shore. I step over a fish carcass. Keep walking along the shoreline, enjoying my inner peace for as long as the pain pills will let me.

I walk over the bridge. Pass the police station. An officer comes out of the front door. I watch him climb into his squad car. I read the words across the car. *To Protect and Serve*.

Those words.

Could they have protected me?

These thoughts are a buzzkill. I walk on. See the church in the distance. I've never been inside a church before. I don't know what to expect. But Pastor Glenn is supposed to be in there. I wonder if he meant what he said about helping me. How can he possibly help me? Still, there is something about him that makes me want to let him try.

I enter the church through a tall red door. I walk through a foyer and into the nave. There are rows and rows of empty pews. They lead up to the altar. White candles are burning on both sides. It's quiet. I walk down the aisle. Should I be in here or not? Maybe he won't remember me. Maybe I'm just another face in the crowd. Maybe he was just being nice. Maybe he wasn't expecting me to take him up on his offer.

Maybe this is a mistake.

I get halfway down the aisle. My doubt overcomes me. I turn to leave.

"Peyton?"

I stop when I hear my name. I turn around. He's standing in the doorway of a room I didn't notice before. I shove my hands into my pockets. Watch him as he walks toward me. I'm suddenly nervous.

"It's good to see you," he says.

"You said you could help me." My stomach churns. I remember what he knows about me. "How?"

He motions to the door. "Come have a seat in my office. We can talk privately."

ભ

Without painkillers? No way could I do this. Pastor Glenn has a friend. She's a detective with the Eastlake Police Department. He drives us over to the building I was afraid to go into on my own. Introduces me to Detective Karen Brown.

Detective Brown takes us into a room. It's just like the ones you see on TV. We sit in the bare room. There's a large wooden table. Chairs. A big mirror on the wall. I stare into the mirror. Wonder if there are people standing in a room on the other side. Are they watching us?

Detective Brown takes a seat across the table from Pastor Glenn and me. She's such a nice woman. Soft-spoken. It's hard to believe she works for the police department. I stare at the table as I recite my story. I'm too ashamed to make eye contact. Detective Brown asks questions. Takes notes on a yellow legal pad. By the time I'm done, she explains to me the details of what should happen. What could happen. What she will try to make happen.

She explains the mistake I made by not reporting the rape right away. Taking a shower. Washing the sheets. Washing away important evidence she could have used to help my case. However, I'm sure I still have the clothes from that night in the bottom of the hamper.

All three of us go back to my house. I dig through the hamper. Bring out the soiled clothes. The detective places them into an evidence bag.

"I know this is hard," she says as she seals the bag. "But can you walk me through that night again?"

Again?

By now it seems like I'm telling the story of someone else. Like I'm telling her about something I saw on TV. Something that didn't really happen. The opposite of what I thought would happen is happening. Instead of being over-whelmed, talking about it makes me feel detached.

We go back to the police station. Back into *the* room. She brings us both a bottle of water. Leaves us. By now my drugs have worn off. Bliss is gone. Peace is gone. My hand hurts. Did I make a mistake? I think Pastor Glenn notices my anxiety.

"This is a mistake. I don't want to do this anymore."

"You made the right decision, Peyton. What you're doing is very brave." He puts a hand on my back. "What that boy did to you was wrong. He was probably count-ing on you to keep quiet. You're doing the right thing. I'm proud of you."

"I don't feel brave." A proud moment? No way. I want to run like a crazy girl. I want out of this building. Want to go home.

Home.

I look at my watch. A new panic sets in. Mom will be home in an hour.

"My mom will be home soon. If I'm not there …"

"I understand. We'll take care of that too. Just relax. Everything will be okay."

೮೩

About an hour later, Detective Brown comes back. Tells us that she picked up Brad. Brought him in for questioning.

He's down the hall from us. Because he's a minor, they're waiting for his parents. They can't question him till then. Now I really start to panic. I feel like I'm the one in trouble. I involved the police.

Pastor Glenn steps out into the hall with Detective Brown. They decide to meet my mom at the house. Leave me here. They'll bring her to me. I am good with that decision.

Another hour goes by. Pastor Glenn opens the door. Mom comes in. Wraps her arms around me.

"Why didn't you tell me?" she whispers. Her eyes are red. So is her nose.

"I'm sorry."

Pastor Glenn comes in next. Acts as my mediator. I let him talk to her. I can't talk without crying. Mom holds my good hand the entire time. A while later Detective Brown comes in. Sits down at the table with us. Fills us in on her interview with Brad. Once his parents arrived, they were able to question him. They didn't get far, though. His parents requested a lawyer. Brad was allowed to leave with his parents.

"We have to wait for the crime lab to process your clothes. Tomorrow I'll go to the clinic and speak with Dr. Cho. Right now all we have is your word against Brad's. Until we have some evidence that a crime was committed, we can't hold him."

"You're letting him go?" Mom gasps.

"We have to." She hands Mom her card. "Once the report comes back from the lab, we can go from there."

"What about school?" I say.

"If he's smart, he will stay away from you. If he doesn't, call me. We can get a restraining order against him."

I look at Mom. She squeezes my hand. "Everything will be okay."

Cs

When we get home, there's an awkward silence between us. I can feel it. Part of me feels ashamed of what happened. Part of me feels closer to Mom. I take my antibiotics and another pain pill. I want that bliss back. It doesn't occur to me to check my phone until I'm ready for bed. I haven't touched it in days.

There are several missed calls and texts from Cassie.

CASSIE: I know ur mad at me. I'm sorry. Can we talk?

CASSIE: I still wanna be your friend. Text me or call me.

CASSIE: What happened? Are you okay? Mr. J said you went to the hospital. Call me.

CASSIE: Peyton, tell me ur ok. Be mad at me. Just tell me ur ok.

CASSIE: What's going on? Cops just took Brad out of class. PLEASE call me.

I stare at my phone. Feel guilty for ignoring her. What's happened to me? She's my best friend. She would never do anything intentionally to hurt me. I stare at the text. All I have to do is tap it. I'll have instant access to her number. Her phone will ring. Why is it so hard? So much has happened. I found some courage.

I feel as if I've aged this past week. Pastor Glenn told me how brave I am. But here I am afraid to call my best friend. I tap her number. Her phone rings. Cassie picks up after two rings.

"Peyton? You okay?"

"Yeah, I'm okay."

Cassie goes on about the police coming to school. Taking Brad out of class. All the rumors that started flying. I fill her in on some of the details, but not all. Then I work my way backward. Explain everything to her. We talk about other stuff too. She even makes me laugh. Leave it to Cassie to make me laugh. Okay, maybe the Vicodin plays a small part. But high on painkillers or not, I love that girl.

CHAPTER 11

I spend most of the weekend avoiding Mom. She knows my dirty secret now. It makes me feel like I've done something wrong. It's hard to avoid her. Whenever I see her, she's too friendly. Babies me. I know she has good intentions. Why does she treat me differently? It only makes me remember the one thing I'm trying to forget. Makes me feel worse.

I go over to Cassie's house for a few hours. I want to hang out. Feel normal. Forget about everything. But then Shane comes home from his football game. He badmouths Brad. Shane's being overly nice. It drives me away too.

I just want people to act normal around me. Stop being over-accommodating. Stop talking to me like I'm a baby. Stop reminding me of what happened.

I go home. Take a pain pill to help me deal with Mom. We rent some movies. Order pizza. Mom never talks during movies or dinner. So two movies and a large pizza guarantee me at least four hours of quiet.

Sunday morning I get dressed. Walk to Pastor Glenn's

church. Mom offers to go with me. But I just want to be alone. I don't know why I want to go. There's something about Pastor Glenn. He makes me feel at ease. Safe. I just want to go see him. See what he does when he's not gluing me back together.

I don't know what time the service started. It has already begun when I arrive. I walk inside. Quietly take a seat in the last pew. A few people turn to look at me. I just smile. Look ahead. Pastor Glenn is in the middle of a sermon.

His voice booms into the microphone. I don't pay attention to his words. I look around at the congregation. Mostly I see the backs of their heads. But I recognize a few of them. A gym teacher from school. A couple of students. I think I see Detective Brown.

I secretly hope no one sees me. I don't want to be recognized. I'm not sure what I want. Why am I here? I don't want to be noticed. But I don't want to go home.

Once the service ends, I'm the first one out the door. I walk down the steps to the prayer garden. There's decorative stonework. The bushes are starting to bud. I bet this will be pretty once the weather breaks. The flowers will bloom. But for now, it's a quiet place to sit.

I sit on one of the four stone benches. The benches circle a ten-foot tall marble statue of the Virgin Mary. My hands are in my pockets. My hood is up. It hides my face and keeps me warm. It's a gloomy Sunday morning. The sky is gray. If it rains, it may turn into snow. Since I'm here, I pray for spring to come.

I watch people file down the steps. They pass the garden. Each time I make eye contact with someone, I pray they will keep moving. Leave me alone. I listen to people talking as they pass. Then car doors close. Cars pull out of the parking lot.

Do these people have perfect lives? Or are they fighting a battle nobody knows about? Like me. The thing I'm trying to forget. The boy's name I try not to say. Or even think about. I wonder if any of them have ever gone through what I've gone through—or maybe worse. Even surrounded by all these people, I feel so alone.

Everyone has gone. I'm ready to leave too. I'm freezing. Nobody will notice me now.

"There you are." Pastor Glenn walks into the garden.

He startles me.

"Are you waiting for someone?" he asks.

"No. I'm just sitting here."

I was hoping to slip away quietly. But maybe I wanted him to find me.

"Did you enjoy the service?" He sits down next to me.

I smile and nod. Is he going to quiz me on it? "I felt a little out of place."

"Was this your first time in a church on a Sunday?"

I nod.

"You're shivering. Come inside. I'll make some hot chocolate for us."

That sounds like a good plan to me.

We go inside. Sit down together. Drink a cup of hot chocolate in the church's kitchen. He gives me a tour and a brief history of the building. His voice is soothing. He talks to me like I'm a normal person. He's not over-the-top. Doesn't baby me. Doesn't talk about what happened. Doesn't bring up anything that makes me remember what I'm trying to forget. He makes me feel safe and welcome.

It is nice.

He takes me home in his warm car. Back to Mom and her endless questions. Her cloying friendliness. She offers me food every hour. Checks on me constantly. Mom is going to drive me crazy with all her good intentions.

Later that day I take my phone off the charger. Turn it on. My nice day is instantly shot to hell.

CHAPTER 12

I have seven missed calls. Twenty-three text messages. What? Is it a mistake? Cassie is the only person who texts me. Something important must have happened. I check my missed calls. Three are from Cassie. The others are from blocked numbers. Most of my text messages are from numbers I don't recognize. I scroll through the messages. My stomach flips with each one.

CASSIE: Call me ASAP!

BLOCKED: Whore.

BLOCKED: Ur a nasty azz skank ho.

CASSIE: Wake up, girl! Call me! 911.

UNKNOWN: Lying slut.

PRIVATE: I hope you die!

UNKNOWN: I'm gonna beat yo ass when I see you.

My phone rings again. I drop it. It hits the floor. Activates the speaker. Crap! A malicious male voice spits out threats.

"I know you're listening, bitch. Check your Facebook.

The whole school knows what a lying ass slut you are. May as well kill yourself now."

I grab my phone. End the call. I go to my Facebook app. My phone rings again. It's Cassie. I answer it immediately.

"Cassie, what's going on?"

"Do *not* go to school tomorrow, girl. Stay home. My notifications have blown up with stuff about you."

"What do they say?"

"Look at your Facebook page."

I go to my desk. Open my laptop. Go straight to my Facebook page. Start reading. I have over one hundred notifications. There is a picture of me with nasty words printed across my face. My school picture has been doctored. My head is attached to a naked body—not mine. There are nasty comments.

Most of the nasty pictures and comments are from football players and cheerleaders. Desi. She hates me. She's the biggest commenter on every post. I can't believe all the mean things she is saying.

Desi Mack: I'm posting Peyton Banks info. Join us in letting the world know what a fat ugly liar she is.
Paige Truman and 13 others like this.

Paige Truman: I second that! I hate liars!
Desi Mack and 11 others like this.

Emily Hart: We should take her fat ass down to the river. Throw her in. One less ugly bitch in the world.
Desi Mack and 14 others like this.

I can't believe what I'm reading. How can so many people hate me? And for what? I'm the victim here. They're talking about me as if I did something wrong.

"Do you see it?" Cassie asks.

"Is this for real?" I say, mostly to myself. "What happened? Why are they doing this?"

"Delete them. Block them. That's what I'm doing."

"They're calling me and texting me too."

"Block them on your phone too, girl."

"Thanks, Cassie." I end the call.

Then I see the comments made by Brad Swisher. My heart drops when I read his comments.

Brad Swisher: Peyton thinks her crap doesn't stink. But that bitch has so many skid marks in her underwear! There's not enough beer to hit that!
Desi Mack and 17 others like this.

Brad Swisher: That bitch practically begged me to take her out. Then she talks smack about me because I wouldn't do her.
Desi Mack and 23 others like this.

I go through my Facebook page. Read. Report. Block. Delete. I change my privacy settings so no one can find me or contact me. This is crazy! Why are they being so mean to me? I'm the victim here.

I toss and turn all night. It's so hard to go to sleep. Those horrible comments! Posted for the world to see. My stomach hurts at the thought of going to school tomorrow. Do I have to face all those mean kids? God, please tell me why this is happening to me?

CHAPTER 13

I sit on my bed. I'm afraid to go to school today. What are my options? I can play sick. Stay home. But then everyone will think I'm scared. I don't want people to think I'm scared—even though I am. I can't let them know I'm afraid.

I look at the clock. I need to make a decision soon. What am I going to tell Mom?

"Peyton, hurry up," Mom calls from downstairs.

Dammit.

I'll just go to school. It may not be as bad as I think. For all I know, these kids can only talk smack on the computer. I doubt they will say anything to my face.

೮ಙ

Is everyone staring at me? I feel like they are as I walk into school. I used to be invisible. Now I feel like all eyes are on me. Groups of kids suddenly stop talking. Stare at me. Whisper behind my back as I pass them in the hall. I avert my eyes. Use my tunnel vision. Focus on reaching my locker.

STICKS AND STONES

I feel threatened. I need to get out of here. Fearing for my own safety, I duck into the restroom. Get away from the menacing looks.

Two girls are putting on makeup in front of the mirror. I recognize them from class. I don't know their names. They stop. Stare at my reflection. I duck into a stall. Take a seat on the edge of the toilet. I slip. Grab at the wall when I almost fall in. For all they know, I just have to pee.

I wait. Listen.

"I wasn't expecting to see her today," girl one says.

"She must be stupid or something," says girl two.

They talk about me as if I'm not in the room. They don't even try to lower their voices.

"I'd be scared if I were her," girl one says.

"She's lucky she didn't get her ass beaten already," says girl two.

They have to know I can hear every word. Are they trying to provoke me? Intimidate me?

Sticks and stones may break my bones, but words will never hurt me. I repeat this in my head. *Sticks and stones. Sticks and stones. Sticks and stones.* It's my mantra. I try to believe it.

I'm scared. A coward. Continue to hide in the stall. Feel like the entire school is against me. I've walked into big trouble. I don't know what to do.

"That bitch will get what's coming to her," girl one says.

They laugh as they leave. I can hear the door open. Voices explode from the hallway. The noise is muffled as the door closes.

I raise my eyes. Notice the writing inside the stall. It's in black marker. My cell number is written below it.

PEYTON BANKS IS A FAT UGLY WHORE

I'm fat? Ugly? A whore? Um, I'm not fat. I don't think I'm ugly. I'm definitely not a whore. But looking at those words? I feel fat. I feel ugly. I feel like a whore.

I leave the stall. I'm alone. I don't want to be afraid, but I am. A sudden chill leaves me cold and shaking. I close my eyes. Take several deep breaths. I'm angry with myself for being afraid. I remember Pastor Glenn telling me how brave I am. I don't feel brave. Why does he think I am? I open my eyes with a new determination.

I will not let these girls—these bullies—scare me.

I won't be controlled like this. The bell will ring soon. I still have to go to my locker. Get my books for first period. I'll hurry. Avoid eye contact with everyone. I'll be okay once I'm in a classroom with a teacher. No one will bother me in front of a teacher. Do the teachers know?

I can hear my name. I don't respond. I get to my locker. The lock is damaged. I pull it off. Open the locker door. I expect to see graffiti. I think my stuff will be gone.

But what I see is so cruel, my heart sinks. I want to vomit. Hanging on a noose is a large dead rat. Its mouth is bloody. Beady eyes stare at me. Something inside me snaps. I start screaming. I look around as I scream. Kids look at me. Some smile or laugh. Others hurry away.

The janitor comes running down the hall. My face is wet and warm. My throat hurts. I can't form words. All I can do is scream. A gym teacher comes running too. He yells at everyone to get to their classes.

Down the hall I can see Brad. He's leaning against his locker, a cocky smile on his face. He turns and walks away.

I spend the first two periods in the principal's office. I calm down. The janitor cleans out my locker. The principal questions me. Promises to launch a full investigation into the vandalism. She's already aware of "the incident" between Brad and me. Knows the police are involved. He is her number one vandalism suspect.

Before she lets me go, she has me talk to the school counselor. Ms. Jaqi is also aware of "the incident." She says she is available to me anytime during school hours. She even gives me some handouts. There is one on date rape. Another is on bullying. There is also a crisis hotline. The same number I got from the clinic. All I want to do is go home.

CHAPTER 14

It's the next day. I don't want to go back to school, but I do. I don't want to face the mean kids and sympathetic teachers, but I do.

I'm afraid to open my locker, but I do. I'm given a new lock. The janitor has done a great job cleaning it out. Disinfecting it. He's even organized my books, folders, and trash. Still, my locker seems dirty and haunted. I don't want this locker anymore. It's ruined.

I try to get through the day without being noticed.

I stay after school. Catch up on my schoolwork. Ms. Fey stays with me to help me out. It only takes me an hour to finish. I stop by my locker on the way out to unload my books. Grab my jacket. It's odd walking these empty halls. It's so quiet. My footsteps seem to echo. They announce my presence to the few people who stayed after school too.

I leave the building. Stand on the school's steps. I can see the football field. I hear the team practicing. The cheerleaders run through their routines. I usually walk past the field on my way home, but not today. No way. The long way adds four blocks to my route. But it's worth it.

I can use the fresh air.

I walk away from the field. Go around the school and through town. I take my time. As I walk toward the park near my house, I can hear music behind me. The sounds of girls talking. I look back. There's a pink convertible. Desi is at the wheel. Paige is in the front passenger seat. The two girls in back are the girls from the restroom. I still don't know their names. I keep walking. They are getting closer. The car slows down.

"Hey, Paige, look at that nasty skank."

Paige laughs.

"Hey, skank," Desi says. "Yeah, you, Peyton Banks. I know you can hear me, you ugly pig."

I try to ignore them. I walk faster. I'm so close to home. Four against one is not fair. Honestly, I'm scared.

"Leave me alone!" I yell. I'm not as threatening as I try to sound.

"You're the one that started this crap about Brad. He's *my* man now."

"You can have him. I don't want him." My voice is shaking.

They pull up ahead of me. Turn into the park entrance. Block my path. I'm not sure if I should turn around or walk faster past them. I just want to go home. I walk faster. Almost run. But they get out of the car and block me.

"Where are you going?" Desi asks. She grabs my bag. Throws it to the ground.

"I'm going home. Leave me alone."

"You're not going anywhere."

All four girls are out of the car. They surround me. Desi grabs me by my hair. Drags me away from the street toward some bushes just inside the park.

I'm grabbing at her hands, trying to get her to let go. But I can't grab anything with my wrapped hand. Suddenly I feel hands all over me. They are hitting me. Smacking me. Punching me. Someone grabs my coat. Pulls it off me. Then someone grabs my shirt. Pulls it up over my head. I can't see. My arms are restricted. I can't fight back.

"Get her hand! Tear her stitches out!"

Someone grabs the bandage on my hand. Rips it off. Steps on my hand. Squishes it into the ground. I scream at the ungodly pain.

"I'll break her damn hand."

"Break her nose too!"

I catch a foot in my stomach. I can't breathe or scream for help. They're cussing at me. Spitting on me. Calling me names. Fingers are digging into the band of my jeans. Fingernails scratch me as they pull my pants down. My jeans catch on my shoes. Bind my feet. I'm completely bound and struggling—half-naked—as they kick me. Hit me. Scratch me. Until finally, I vomit.

"You bitch! You puked on my shoes!"

I don't know whose voice that is.

"She puked on my shoes!"

"Kick her in the face!"

There is a kick to my head. A bright flash of light. I get woozy. I close my eyes. Grab my head the best I can. I hear a commotion. The girls retreat quickly. I can hear their footsteps running for Desi's car. Tires screech. They speed off.

I hear footsteps running toward me. I'm scared I'll get hit again.

"Are you okay?" a deep male voice asks.

I can feel large hands touching me. Pulling my shirt down. Releasing my arms. The man is kneeling beside me. He wraps his jacket around me. I lean against his chest. Finally someone has come to my rescue.

"I need an ambulance at Stratton Park. A girl was attacked."

Oh God, he's calling for help. People are going to come. See me half-naked. I reach down. Struggle with my jeans. Try to pull them up. I'm so embarrassed this man has seen me in my underwear. I can't even look at him.

"Hold on. I'll help you."

CHAPTER 14

I see his hands come toward me. I move away from him, shaking my head. "I can do it. I don't need help."

It's hard, but I get to my feet. Pull up my jeans. Straighten out my clothes. Once I think I have myself together, I feel queasy. Fall to my knees. I want to puke again.

"Sit down and relax. Help is coming."

Within minutes I hear sirens in the distance. The sound grows louder and louder. I watch the man's shadow as he walks to the street. Flags down help. My vision is blurry. But I think there's a police car and an ambulance. I hear the man talking to the police. Says he lives down the street. Heard a commotion. Walked down to see what was going on.

Another officer is asking me questions as the paramedics clean me up. They are going to take me to the hospital. I don't want to go back there. But my stitches tore open. My hand is battered and bleeding. Is it broken?

I tell the officer what happened. Give them the girls' names, the ones I knew of anyway. I give descriptions of the other two girls. Then I'm on my way to the hospital.

I'm waiting in the emergency room for Mom to come get me. A nurse peeks around the curtain.

"You have a visitor," she says.

Thinking it's Mom, I slide off the bed. Get ready to go. Then a large black man comes in. He's holding my coat and backpack.

"I think these belong to you," he says.

I don't recognize him at first, but I recognize his voice. He's the man from the park. My rescuer. A hero.

"Thank you." I take my things from him. "I'm sorry I didn't thank you for helping me before."

"It's all right. I'm just glad you're okay."

I hear another voice outside the curtain. Pastor Glenn steps in. He looks at me. Then he looks at the man. "So, you're this young lady's hero?"

The man smiles. Shakes hands with him. "How you doing, Pastor Glenn?"

"I'm doing fine, Reggie. May the Lord bless you for helping this young lady."

Apparently they know each other. That's how it is when you live in a small town. I sit back on the bed. Listen as they talk about the incident, then about church. Reggie says goodbye and leaves.

"How did you know I was here?"

"I was visiting patients when Detective Brown called me. She filled me in on what happened. How are you feeling?"

"I feel like crap."

"Will it make you feel better to know that those girls are being arrested as we speak?"

I can't say it makes me feel better. Actually, I'm not sure how I feel about it. I know those girls have parents with a lot of money. I'm sure they will be out on bail in no time. At some point I'll have to face them at school. How can I even think about going back to school after all this?

Before I can respond to his question, Mom comes through the curtain.

"What happened?" She looks like she's about to freak out.

I tell Mom everything that happened. Pastor Glenn tells her what he told me.

"You should go down to the police station. Speak with Detective Brown," he tells Mom.

"We will be pressing charges against those girls. This is ridiculous! Awful."

And that's exactly what we do.

We spend two hours in the police station. We talk to Detective Brown. Fill out paperwork. I'm taken to a room with a glass window. I can see in. The people on the other side cannot see out. I identify my attackers. Even behind bars, the girls look scary.

CHAPTER 15

I stay home from school. Mom insists. Fine with me. I spend most of the day watching TV. Texting with Cassie. I get a few more text messages from blocked numbers. Numbers I don't recognize. I delete them without reading them. I don't want to know what they say.

I get on the computer. Look at my Facebook page. There are nasty comments and messages there too. I go through them one by one. Block and report the people who are harassing me. Someone can always find a way to say something mean to me. But I'm not going to completely disappear because of stupid bullies.

Cassie comes over after school. Brings my books and homework. We do our work together. Then Mom comes home and orders pizza. Cassie fills me in on all the rumors going around school. Word is out that those girls were arrested. They may get kicked off the cheerleading squad for assaulting me. The school has zero tolerance against bullying.

A part of me feels bad for them. But not that bad. They had a lot to lose. Mostly I feel happy they are being punished. They only have themselves to blame for what they did to me. No one forced them to beat me up. They have to suffer the consequences of their actions.

Cassie also said there is a rumor that Brad may get kicked off the football team. The only reason he is still playing is because he hasn't been charged with anything. Without Brad our team will suffer in the play-offs. Losing the most experienced cheerleaders may cost our team the state competition. Do I care? I'm not sure.

We have a good time hanging out. Then Mom takes her home. It feels good to not be mad at Cassie anymore. I don't have to avoid her. She understands me. She gave me my space. Waited for me to be ready for her again. That's why she's my best friend.

CHAPTER 16

I stay home from school another day. Mom's at work. I have the house to myself. I decide to be as unproductive as possible. It's only nine in the morning, but I'm still in my jammies. I'm chilling on the couch. Texting Cassie. Then the doorbell rings. I think about not answering. I don't want to be bothered. Then it rings again.

I get up. Tiptoe to the window. Peek out the blinds. Who is standing on my porch? When I can't see anyone, I sneak up to the door. Peek out the door's tiny window. It's Tammy Davison. But why? I never talk to her. Why isn't she in school? I don't have anything to say to her. Why is she here?

She looks up. We make eye contact. Dammit. There goes my sneakiness.

"Who is it?" I don't know why I say this. I already know who it is.

"It's Tammy from school. Is that you, Peyton?"

Did she come here to beat me up too? I don't think so.

She's pregnant. As far as I know, she has nothing to do with those other girls. Or anyone else, for that matter.

"Yeah, why?"

I still don't want to open the door. I don't want to get into a fight with a pregnant girl.

"Can we talk?" Her voice is shaky. Unsure.

She doesn't seem like a threat. I feel silly for even thinking she would punch me. So I unlock the door and open it. She's standing there in her second-hand maternity clothes. Her hair is pulled back into a messy ponytail. She looks so tired and harmless.

"Why aren't you in school?" I ask through the screen door.

"I have a doctor's appointment today. Can I come in?"

I look her over once more. She seems harmless. I open the door. Let her in. We go into the living room. I motion for her to have a seat. She puts her backpack on the couch. Takes off her coat. Maneuvers herself into a sitting position. Her belly is so big. She looks really uncomfortable.

"Did you walk here?" I ask.

"Yeah. I was on my way to the health clinic. I wanted to stop by and see if you're okay."

I can tell she feels as awkward as I do. She keeps looking at the TV. I turn the volume down a little so we can get to the point of her visit. I sit down on the arm of a recliner across from her.

"I'm fine. I just need some time to myself. What do you want to talk about?"

"It's going around school that Brad raped you."

"Why would I talk to you about this? It's none of your business." Suddenly agitated, I get up. Go to the door and hold it open. "I don't wanna talk about this with you."

She doesn't move. She just sits there looking at me. Like she can't take the hint that I want her to leave.

"I'm not here to make you mad, Peyton. This isn't easy for me either."

"What are you talking about?"

"You're not the only one." She puts her hands on her belly and looks away.

There's a warm sickening feeling in the pit of my stomach.

"What are you saying?" I already have an idea of what she's saying. But I want to hear it from her.

"Eight months ago, Brad asked me out on a date. We went to a movie. Then we went back to his place." She didn't look at me when she spoke. She looked everywhere but at me. "His dad has a refrigerator full of beer in his garage. His parents weren't home. I don't think his parents are ever home. We hung out and drank beer. I only had one. It made me sick. I wanted to leave. He said I could lie down in his room until I felt better. And then …"

My hand drops from the doorknob. I take a few steps

toward her. Eight months ago? I look at her belly. "Is that his baby?"

She nods. Wipes tears from her eyes. I shut the door. Go to the bathroom and get her a box of tissues. Then I sit down next to her.

"You're so lucky you didn't get pregnant. Do you have any idea what it's like to be pregnant with his baby? I don't want it. I can't wait until I have it so I can get rid of it. It's a constant reminder of that night. I just want it to go away."

Am I lucky? I don't feel so lucky.

"You didn't tell anyone?"

She shakes her head. "I didn't think anyone would believe me because he's the nice guy. I'm the girl that screws the football team. I only had sex with one other person. Ever. But everyone calls me a slut. Says I'll screw anybody for a beer."

I remember all the things I've heard about her. All the things I believed were true. I wonder if those same people are saying those things about me now. I look at her and think this could be me. I can't imagine having to carry the baby of my rapist for nine months. Having to see him every day at school. I don't know how she does it.

"Did he give you chlamydia too?"

This takes me for a loop. "What? No. I don't think so."

"Did you get tested?"

"No." I didn't think I had to.

"You should. It took about two weeks before I showed any symptoms. Even then I waited a couple more weeks before I went to the clinic. That's when I found out I was pregnant too."

This poor girl now has me worried. She's had to suffer through a pregnancy and an STD. I already took care of the pregnancy part. Well, I think I did anyway. I never thought about getting a disease.

"You didn't know about the Plan B pill?"

"I didn't know about it until it was too late. My mom didn't have the money for an abortion. I have an appointment with an adoption agency in Chicago next week. I get to pick a good family for the baby."

I'm looking at this girl. The quiet outcast I've heard so many rumors about. I formed an opinion about her based on those rumors. But those rumors are lies. I based my opinion on those lies. How many others have done the same thing? Treating her like an outcast. Talking trash about her based on lies. Now I feel guilty for being one of those people.

I feel bad for her. Maybe because we're both in the same boat. How many people are listening to lies about me? Judging me by those lies?

"I'm going down to the clinic for my check-up. Do you want to come with me and get tested?"

I dread going back to that horrid place. But she's right.

I do need to get tested for STDs. While I'm there, I may as well get that pregnancy test done. Make sure I'm out of the woods. Going back may be easier now since I don't have to go alone. I guess when you're in the same boat, it's best to stay together.

"I don't wanna go, but I will."

☃

Another forty-degree day makes the long walk almost pleasant. Tammy and I get to know each other. She is actually a pretty cool person. We have a lot of things in common. I can totally see us being friends.

My second time at the health clinic isn't as bad as the first. I think it's because this time Tammy is here. Having her with me brings me some comfort. I think she feels better knowing she has a shoulder to lean on too.

I never thought about it before. It must be pretty lonely going through a pregnancy with no support. Tammy doesn't have any friends. No one wants to be friends with a pregnant girl. Nobody's parents want their kids hanging around a pregnant girl. Her reputation is based on lies. That sucks for her. Her mom works two jobs just to make ends meet. Her older brother is never home.

The wait isn't as long this time. Since we've both been here before, we don't have to fill out any forms again.

We go back in the same group. We each have our own exam room. Once again I change into the flimsy gown.

Cover myself with the paper towel I'm given. Wait for Dr. Cho.

First I have to pee into a cup. Then I have to go through that horrible pelvic exam again. The entire time I'm lying there, I'm searching the ceiling for that little spider.

"Did you talk to Detective Brown?" I ask as soon as he is done.

"Yes, I did."

"You knew, didn't you?"

"Yes, I did." He finishes making his notes. "She asked for your medical records to help with your case. I can't release your records without your permission or a subpoena. However, I can give you a copy of your medical records if you sign a release form."

"Then I can give them to her?"

"They're your records You can do what you want with them."

It takes me a moment to realize he's trying to help me without telling me what to do. If I can get my records and Tammy can get hers, we can give them to Detective Brown. It will help her move this case along. I just want this nightmare to be over with. I want to move forward with my life.

ℭℬ

The pregnancy test comes back negative. What a big relief. I really dodged a bullet there. But I'm careful not to make such a big deal out of it in front of Tammy. She wasn't as lucky as me. Even when she expresses her happiness for me, I detect a little jealousy. The STD test comes back positive for chlamydia. My heart sinks at the thought of having an STD. Gross. It makes me feel dirty again.

It was caught early. Before I showed any symptoms. I thank Tammy for that. I would never have guessed to get checked for it if she didn't tell me. Who knows how long it would have gone undetected? Or what would have happened if I had let it go untreated? Scary.

They give me a prescription for antibiotics. Stronger than the ones I am taking for my hand. The drugs should clear it up. I come back in two weeks to get retested. Are you kidding me? Oh well.

I talk with Tammy about what we should do. We both sign the release papers for our medical records.

ঙ

We walk across town. A bitter wind blows in from the north. But the sun at our backs gives some comfort and warmth. We spent almost four hours at the health clinic. When I mention how hungry I am, Tammy pulls out a bag of cookies from her backpack. I only take a few cookies. Just enough to quiet the rumbling in my belly. Tammy needs them more.

As we approach the police station, she stops.

"I don't know if I can do this, Peyton."

I look at her. I remember feeling the same way. When Pastor Glenn encouraged me to talk to the police, I told myself I couldn't. Throughout the entire interview with Detective Brown, I told myself I couldn't. When the police brought Brad in, I told myself I couldn't. When Mom came in and put her arms around me? I realized I *am* doing this.

I take Tammy's hand. Give it a squeeze. "You *can* do this."

I see the relief wash over her face. She smiles. Squeezes my hand back. Together we walk into the Eastlake Police Department. I introduce her to Detective Karen Brown.

CHAPTER 17

Brad Swisher's arrest makes the front page of the local newspaper. It's no secret who his accusers are. His friends either avoid us or give us dirty looks as they pass us in the hallway. It's odd to feel like an outsider. But Tammy, Cassie, and I have our own clique. Shane is on the fence. He tries to balance his loyalty for his team, friends, and family.

ဢ

The first couple days after Brad's arrest were rough. Then something happened. Another girl came forward. Amanda Jefferies. She was a promising gymnast. The athletic blonde dropped out of school after the Valentine's Day dance. No one has spoken about her since.

She claimed the rape took place the night of the dance. Refused to return to school afterward. Two weeks later she was treated for chlamydia. Four weeks after that, she had an abortion.

For a while it seemed as if it was just the three of us. Then two more girls from another school came forward.

Brad stayed in jail for a week. Then his parents were able to take out a second mortgage to post his bail. They used the rest of the money to hire the best lawyer their money could buy.

Brad came to school long enough to find out he was dropped from the football team. He was shunned. Even his former teammates wanted nothing to do with him anymore. He cleaned out his locker and stormed out of the school.

We all had our day in court. Facing our attacker and reliving the nightmare was tough. I cried in the witness box as I told my story. I went first. It was really hard! But I think my testimony gave strength to the other girls so they could do the same.

It took the jury almost two hours to deliberate. Guilty on all counts. Brad was tried as an adult. He was sentenced to jail. Fifteen to twenty-five years. Plus, he has to register as a sex offender when he gets out.

Desi Mack and the other girls pleaded guilty to assault. They were tried as adults too. Sentenced to six months in jail plus two hundred hours of community service. Of course they were kicked off the cheerleading squad. Desi lost her college scholarship as well.

Our school took a hit. That year the Eastlake Eagles lost the final game 6–33 against the Parkway Steelmen. Our cheerleaders came in last at the state competition.

I remember when Pastor Glenn told me everything

happens for a reason. This includes the good, the bad, and the ugly. Violence lead me to Pastor Glenn. He made me realize how strong I was. My courage gave Tammy courage. Three other girls came forward. We put our rapist in jail. We made new friendships and prevented future crimes.

I introduced Tammy to Pastor Glenn. He happened to know a young married couple that wanted to adopt a baby. Pastor Glenn has known Robert and Nora Drake since they were kids. He even married them in his church. The Drakes had successful careers and a nice home. But they were unable to have children of their own. Not only did they pay for Tammy's medical expenses, but they also invested money toward her college education.

Amanda Jeffries re-enrolled in school to finish off her senior year. It was hard for her at first. Everyone treated her like an outcast. Hounded her with questions. But then she joined our little clique. After a couple weeks, kids started leaving her alone.

Pastor Glenn formed a rape-counseling group. The group met once a week in the church's basement. Most of us attended on a regular basis. The group gave us a safe place to talk. It also helped knowing I wasn't the only one. Having support—and giving support—helped me to heal.

Healing is a process.

Even through the darkest times, there was light. Some good came out of the bad. We faced our rapist in court. Put him away. Got justice for others. Prevented future crimes. Made new friends. Tammy answered the Drakes' prayers. Gave them a baby they could love. She worked harder in school because she knew she could afford college.

And me? Sticks and stones may break my bones, but I will never let the words of bullies hurt me.

Because I'm better than that.

WANT TO KEEP
READING?

Turn the page for a sneak peek at another book from the Gravel Road Rural series: M.G. Higgins's *Roadside Attraction.*

ISBN: 978-1-68021-102-3

Chapter 1

My dad always says, "You've seen one cactus. You've seen them all."

I get his point. But at least the cactus are interesting. More interesting than the plants where we live. Knee-high brush that's kindling by August.

Tumbling tumbleweeds.

Those are words from an old song. The kind of music my grandparents play at their store. Like there's something romantic about tumbleweeds. Stuck in cattle fences, jammed under junk cars.

I don't like disagreeing with my dad. But I like cactus. Especially saguaros, the tall green ones I'm driving by right now. They look like giant cactus people. Arms out. Palms up. Like they're being arrested. "Stick 'em up, cactus *hombre*." Mom took me to a park around here when I was ten. There were a zillion of them. A cactus convention.

The highway curves and the cactus people disappear.

Tucson recedes in my rearview mirror. Traffic thins out. Now it's just me. Semis. RVs. Cars loaded with tents and suitcases. Kids in the backseat, whining, "Are we there yet?"

All those travelers equal money in my grandparents' pockets. Which equals money in my pockets. So I don't complain. I like the money I make. Can't wait to spend it on something now that I've graduated.

The landscape turns flat and barren. Distant mountains. Tumbleweeds not tumbling in the hot still air.

An hour later things get rockier. The signs start showing up. *Geronimo's Last Stand! Ten Miles Ahead!*

Two miles later: *Geronimo's Last Stand! See History! Gas! Sodas! Snacks! Souvenirs!*

I've just passed *Authentic Mexican Pottery! Geronimo's Last Stand! 2 Miles!* when I see a hitchhiker. Short cut-off jeans. Backpack. Thumb out.

Our eyes meet as I drive by. She's young, maybe fourteen or fifteen. Frowning. Short black hair with blue streaks. Flip-flops. No hat. It's over a hundred degrees. What is she thinking?

There's no way I'm picking her up. Never picked up a hitchhiker. Never will. I've heard too many horror stories. Seen too many freaky movies.

I turn up the radio. Flex my fingers around the steering wheel. Reach the final billboard two miles later. *Geronimo's Last Stand. THIS EXIT!!!! TURN NOW!!!!*

I turn and take the exit. But not because the sign tells me to.

I belong here.

The parking lot is full. Gas pumps busy. The facade of the convenience store looks like a town from the Old West. It's just a front. Fake. Supposed to add to the old-timey atmosphere.

I drive to the rear. Park next to the loading door. Grab two cardboard boxes from the back of the pickup and carry them to the storeroom.

Grandpa meets me there. "Hey, Logan. Did they hassle you about the return?"

"No, they were cool."

He grabs the box cutter from the workbench. Cuts through the packing tape and pulls out a T-shirt. It's bright blue. Outline of Geronimo's face in dark green. Green lettering underneath. *Geronimo's Last Stand. Ferris, Arizona.*

He studies it and nods. "Better than the last batch." He opens the other box. "Did you go see your mom?"

"No."

"But you said—"

"I never said anything. You assumed, like always."

He sighs and shakes his head. Pulls out a baseball cap. Same blue as the shirts. Same lettering and image. "Stock a few shirts in the store, will you? Especially extra large. We sold the last one this morning. Then we can use your help at the registers. I need to watch for a delivery."

I carry a bunch of T-shirts into the store. Stack them on the shelves. The clothing aisle is near the restrooms. A string of women line up outside the ladies room. That's why most people stop here—to pee. But almost no one leaves without buying something, even if it's just a soda. Bag of chips. And they want to see Geronimo's Last Stand, of course. All those billboards stoke their curiosity.

"Logan!" Grandma waves me over to the counter. Customers wait six deep behind her register.

I go over and help her. "Where's Dad?"

"Taking a break."

Dad needs a lot of breaks. He's not really suited for this kind of work. But there's not a lot else he can do. "Is he okay?" I ask.

"Just a bad day."

I shouldn't have gone to Tucson. It upset his routine.

I notice Melody get in my line. She's holding Hannah, her baby daughter.

"I can help you over here, sweetie," Grandma says to her. My line's moving slower.

"That's okay, Mrs. Monroe." Melody flashes her sweet smile that makes my insides melt. Her light brown hair is pulled back in her summer ponytail.

I finish with my customer. Melody sets a Diet Coke

on the counter. Bag of pretzels. She shifts Hannah on her hip.

"No Snickers today?" I ask.

"I'm on a diet."

"You're kidding."

"I've turned pudgy since Hannah, as if you haven't noticed. Hey, have you heard from Seth?"

I shake my head.

"Neither have we. Thought he might have texted you."

"He just left Sunday. I'm giving him a chance to settle in," I say.

"That's what I told Mom and Dad. But …" she shrugs. "They worry."

I give Melody her change.

"You working here all summer?" she asks.

"Nothing else to do. Not with Seth at baseball camp." I bag her stuff. Hand it to her.

"Well, see you around," she says.

"Right. See you later."

My eyes linger on her as she leaves with Hannah. She's not fat. She's perfect. A girl passes them coming into the store. Black hair with blue streaks. Cut-off blue jeans. Flip-flops.

The hitchhiker.

She scans us. I don't think she recognizes me. Not that she would. I drove by at eighty miles an hour. She's carrying that big backpack. Perfect for shoplifting.

The registers have slowed. "Think I'll follow that one," I whisper to Grandma.

She studies the girl, same as I did. "Might want to get your dad up here first."

I head to the staff room. It's just a small space with a couch and card table. Coffee maker and small refrigerator. Broken souvenirs, or ones that never sold—fake kachina dolls, fake Indian blankets. A desert wildflower poster. Dad's sitting at the table, hands folded in front of him. He jerks his head up when I walk in. Gives me a relieved smile. "You're back."

"Of course I'm back. Feel good enough to go up front?"

"Sure. Is it busy?"

"Not bad. Possible shoplifter I need to watch."

"Then go ahead." His knees shake as he gets to his feet.

"Are you sure? I can drive you home."

"I'm fine!"

I give him a final glance before I go to the storeroom. Grab a handful of baseball caps. They'll give me a reason to walk the aisles.

I look up at the fish-eye mirror near the ceiling. Don't see the girl. Maybe she's in the restroom. I stock the caps on the shelf, next to the snow globes and collector spoons. She leaves the restroom just as I finish. I wander slowly behind her.

A car backfires outside.

Someone screams.

It's Dad.

ABOUT DATE RAPE
(from *girlshealth.gov*)

Rape is a crime. It is sex you don't agree to. Date rape is when you are raped by someone you know, like a boyfriend. Rape is always wrong. Even if you were drinking, it is not your fault.

Who can I call for help?
If you have been sexually assaulted, go to an emergency room. If you want to report the rape to the police, do not shower, change clothes, or brush your teeth. There are also free hotlines that you can call. The lines are open 24 hours a day.

There are also hotlines if you need advice on how to leave an unhealthy relationship. There are also local resources, like women's shelters or other services, through your local phone book, a religious center, your school counselor or nurse, or a doctor's office.

National Sexual Assault Hotline
1-800-656-HOPE (1-800-656-4673)

National Domestic Violence Hotline
1-800-799-SAFE (1-800-799-7233) or
1-800-787-3224 (TDD)

Girls and Boys Town National Hotline
1-800-448-3000 or 1-800-448-1833 (TDD)

ABOUT THE AUTHOR

Donna Shelton is an award-winning poet and author. Born in Chicago, she has had over 200 short stories, poems, and articles published since she began writing as a child. Shelton's first novel, *Breaking Dawn*, was published in 2012. The book was nominated for a YALSA Quick Pick for Reluctant Young Readers. Shelton lives in Morris, Illinois, and is a single mother with two children and many rescued pets. For more information about Shelton and her other books, check out her website at www.donnashelton.weebly.com.

ABOUT THE AUTHOR